Who Is My Neighbor?

Who Is My Neighbor?

Stories by

Minta Sue Berry

THE UNIVERSITY OF TENNESSEE PRESS / KNOXVILLE

The paper used in this book meets the minimum
requirements of ANSI/NISO Z39.48-1992 (R 1997)
(Permanence of Paper). The binding materials have
been chosen for strength and durability.

Library of Congress Cataloging-in-Publication Data

Berry, Minta Sue, 1931–
Who is my neighbor? / Minta Sue Berry.— 1st ed.
    p. cm.
ISBN 1-57233-115-1 (cl.: alk. paper)
1. Southern States—Social life and customs—
Fiction. I. Title.
PS3552.E7477 W48 2001
813'.54—dc21
                                        00-010298

*W*ith gratitude to my parents and sisters for their encouragement and influence; to my teachers who fostered my love for words—Mildred Ferrell Bassham and George Worley Boswell; and to Walter Sullivan, whose Creative Writing class at Vanderbilt developed in me the means and the determination to write fiction.

Contents

Warring with Old Enemies

Next-Door Neighbors

*E*mma Simpkins was working in her garden when the news came that President Roosevelt had died. Not that there was anything to tend yet, for she stubbornly refused to let her husband Will talk her into planting before the middle of April, and that was a good week away.

"Get them tender little plants up and then here comes a killin' frost and cuts them to the ground," she insisted. "We don't have enough empty fruit jars to turn down over every little bean and pea up and down the rows. I can't stand to watch them get bit. We'll just wait for the right time."

But she didn't mean sit and wait. So on that afternoon when Miss Maisie came up the road to bring the awful word, she was busy getting ready for a new crop. She was methodically picking up, one at a time, bean sticks that had been pulled down in the fall and piled, helter-skelter, near the garden fence. Each spring, as today, she stripped away the remnants of crackly dead vines still clinging to the poles and then stood them neatly in a fence corner, where they looked like gray spear shafts, only so spindly that it was hard to believe that in a matter of weeks they would be once more supporting black-green leaves so rank that she had to keep warning the children of the deadly copperheads that liked to hide under them. Already, she was thinking of those hateful intruders that were a threat to her babies, and she threw a cleaned stick hard in the direction of the growing pile just as her eye caught a glimpse of Miss Maisie rushing up the road, not sauntering with one hand on a hip, the way she usually did.

"Oh, Lord," she said in a loud, frightened tone, standing up straight and dropping a stick to the ground. Old Kaiser Bill, startled, quivered, and then shook out, simultaneously, the dust from his sleek, cinnamon-colored skin and the sun-dreams from his dog brain. He cast an irate side-glance at Emma and limped on his three good legs to a more peaceful couch.

Genny and Myrtle Lou looked up at their mother, startled. On hands and knees in the almost powdery brown dirt, they had been busily "planting" and "unplanting" marbles, counting carefully so as not to leave a single one buried when the game was through. Genny, who was eight, was in charge of keeping count as well as deciding the identity of each "plant." Both were liberally sprinkled from head to toe and totally grimy from blackened fingernails to elbows. They had been largely unaware of all but their engrossing activity until their mother spoke.

"Oh, Lord," she repeated, wiping her hands on the front of her dress and starting hurriedly toward the garden gate, while Miss Maisie was getting nearer as fast as she could.

"She must have got word about one of her boys," she said to herself, but this time the girls heard clearly, and they stood up, scared.

By the time Emma had stumbled and stepped over the hard clods to the gate and fumbled with the rusty chain, Miss Maisie was close enough that her loud, heaving pants and a kind of wordless groan could be heard.

Emma had to go only a few steps down the road to meet her aging neighbor, who halted in her tracks and, now that she was near enough to speak, could only wheeze and open and close her mouth like a fish gasping for air, looking all the while hopelessly up from her short stature into the now pale face of Emma, who placed her arm around her shoulders and steered her toward the yard, both of them for the moment wordless. Getting her thus far, she stood facing her there where yellow-green was already beginning to win over bleak, winter brown. She made another appeal.

"Miss Maisie, please, what on earth's the matter? Can't you tell us?" She shook her gently and looked pleadingly into the lined old face. She saw that her eyes were red around the rims, and a few big tears stalled amid the network of wrinkles that criss-crossed her cheeks.

"Is it about Sambo or Junior?" she persisted because she had to, though reluctant to put the fearful suspicion into words. But even before Miss Maisie shook her head in denial, shivering a little, Emma knew that couldn't be it: the ancient eyes looked frightened and sad, not hopeless and destroyed as they would if one of her boys had been reported missing or dead. Besides, Emma now realized, feeling somewhat foolish in spite of her great concern, if the War Department had delivered such a message, Miss Maisie would not have been the one to bring the word to her neighbors.

That left her still wondering, what? Was it something to do with her own family? Instinctively she glanced around to assure herself of the children's safety. No, there they were, a study of varying degrees of curiosity: Myrtle Lou peeping from behind her mother's print dress tail, one hand making and unmaking a fistful of wadded, faded apron; Genny equally curious, but a bit more aloof, leaning against the trunk of the old maple, beside the zinc tub in which her new pet, an injured English sparrow, thrashed against a rusty window screen which completed its cage; Kaiser Bill making whistling noises as he snuffled at Miss Maisie's dusty, run-over shoes. It was obvious that all would have reached out to take from her what it was Miss Maisie would have told, had in fact come to tell, but, once here, was incapable of beginning. It was as if she had practiced a speech to say, had said it over and over to herself every step of the way, had imagined their reactions, until now it was old, too old to tell; it seemed that it was all finished, ages ago, and she could not endure tasting the words again.

"Did Sambo get dead, Mama?" Myrtle Lou whimpered, her words almost smothered against her mother's leg. He was her favorite: when he was home on furlough, visiting Miss Maisie, he had ridden her on his shoulders, trotting like a wild horse until his round, white sailor cap had tumbled off into the grass.

"No, Hon, be quiet," her mother replied, low, reaching down and touching her head lightly. Emma was aware of the softness of Myrtle Lou's fine hair, of the whack of Will's axe from over the hill where he was clearing ground for a plant bed, of fluffy spurts of gray smoke floating from the brush fires he had set. She even thought how good that the air was still; there was no danger of the fire getting out and, maybe, causing Will to be hurt. All the time she was aware that Miss Maisie was breathing more easily and was moving her lips finally to speak.

She began by wiping her nose with a quick sweep of the back of her hand. When words finally broke through, her tone was wet-sounding, but cold and matter-of-fact as though she were announcing something ordinary and insignificant, like, "The wind has shifted to the north."

"The president's dead. President Roosevelt is dead."

Emma blinked her eyes and didn't say a word. She just stood there, quiet, turning a little pale, and stared at Miss Maisie as if what she had told was intensely interesting, even amazing, but certainly not true. Her seemingly calm reaction served to make Miss Maisie feel the need to respond with more emotional force. Putting both of her brown puffy, age-spotted hands to her face, she began to cry; and her short, heavy body shook with almost soundless anguish.

Genny crept nearer, to stand close to her mother, amazed at the old woman's crying at all, and particularly at her doing so without the loud wails that unfailingly accompanied her own weeping, or that of Myrtle Lou or little Budge. She unconsciously rubbed the sole of her left foot up and down her right calf and stared, entranced, as tears seeped through Miss Maisie's fingers and trickled toward her wrists.

She had heard what Miss Maisie said: President Roosevelt was dead. Through her mind flashed the image of an old man sitting in front of a fireplace talking about far-off places and serious things. Sometimes he talked to his people over the radio, and all of the children knew to be quiet or go play in another room while the grown-ups pulled straight chairs close to the big cabinet radio, listening quietly and looking mostly at the floor until he finally said, in that important sounding voice, "Good night." Then Papa would reach over and snap the button off, and they would sit for a while talking in hushed tones, as if they were in church.

When Granny was there, she would always say, "He'd better watch out for them Russians. They're the ones that're gonna get us, if I know my Bible." And she would shake her head, as if she could already see some catastrophe looming, just waiting for the president to turn his head. But Papa would say, "FDR knows his business, Mama," and then get up and go outside to see to the cows or get a fresh stick of wood for the fire.

Genny was sorry he was dead. She remembered the sound of his voice—like the peddler's that came by on Tuesdays and sometimes let her and Myrtle Lou choose an all-day sucker apiece; only the president talked more proper because he lived in the city and talked on the radio—and was a president besides.

"Miss Maisie," Genny heard her mother saying now, "let's go inside for awhile. You'll make yourself sick standin' there cryin' like that. You've done wore yourself out with running almost to tell us and all." She was gently trying to turn Miss Maisie's big clumsy body and steer her up the path to the porch.

Miss Maisie quit heaving so violently and took her hands from her face, clasping Emma's wrist wetly. "Emma, you better thank the good Lord you ain't got no boys over yonder. Sambo's across the waters and maybe miring up in some sloppy ditch this minute and Junior's floatin' around Lord knows where on that awful ocean, and the president's dead, and, oh, Emmie, now I ain't got more'n a drop of hope of ever seein' them again." She started again, and this time Emma, after glancing once at the puffs of smoke rising above the hills, firmly began to guide the older woman through the yard to the porch.

Genny stooped to lift the screen from the tub and take out Crippy Crow, her sparrow bird that was scarcely crippled at all anymore. She held him lovingly against her neck as she watched the disorderly procession move to the porch of the gray log house. Miss Maisie wasn't watching where she walked, and she stepped between most of the limestone rocks that marked the path up to the steps. Once, she almost stumbled on the edge of one of them, and as Emma caught and steadied her, an old dominecker hen that had wallowed out a dust nest under a lilac bush became startled and squawked off to another part of the yard, leaving a few speckled feathers to float slowly to the grass.

"Watch that old bottom step, Miss Maisie; it's half rotten," Genny heard her mother say.

Myrtle Lou had run ahead of the women, and, as the planks creaked beneath Miss Maisie's mounting hulk, she leaned toward her, hanging precariously by one arm which was hooked around a post. "Mama, is President Rosie Belle kin to Miss Maisie? Why is she crying?"

She looked puzzled and disappointed when her mother ignored the question and told her to open the screen door. She obeyed, and the three of them disappeared into the darkness of the living room. Genny knew, before it happened, that they wouldn't stop on the porch. Somehow, the occasion seemed altogether too special to be acted out anywhere besides in the room where they always took the preacher and other impor-tant people. She had to see what was going to take place, so she scooped up her bird and ran inside too.

It was quiet in the cool, dim room. The two women were not chattering about their gardening plans or swapping settings of eggs, as they usually did; they were just sitting—Miss Maisie fitted into the best stuffed rocking chair, with her feet barely touching the floor, and Emma in the straight chair with arms, sitting stiff and tall as if she were visiting in someone else's parlor. The only sounds were of little Budge's deep, regular breathing from the dusky back corner of the room, where he lay huddled on his stomach in a big brown box whose sides had been cut down to make a playpen; and an occasional squeak of Myrtle Lou's knees against the slick linoleum as she moved about her mother's chair, plaiting and unplaiting the fringe that hung from the seat.

Genny took her bird and sat flat on the floor near Budge's pen. With one finger she gently traced the square black letters on the side of the box. They spelled out "Cozy Morning Heater," and just above them upside down in smeared yellow crayon marks, "Here lies Budge." Not long ago, she had scrawled those words herself and then placed the box over little Budge and waited for her mother to come into the room and appreciate the huge joke. She came, and she read the yellow words slowly, moving her lips, but she looked angry instead of amused—frightened, even; and she went out back by the clothes line and returned with a peach tree switch to stripe her legs. Genny wondered about that a little now, as she listened to the silence a-buzz in the room and in her ears and smelled the sweet aroma of honeysuckle floating from the quart fruit jar on the top of the old organ. Then Miss Maisie began to talk.

"Yes, President Roosevelt is dead." She said the words not as if to inform—she had already done that—but as though she was compelled to bring the fact into the room with them, to fill the air with the shock and the threat.

"Yes'm—it's hard to believe." Emma leaned over and picked up the black family Bible from the table near her, absent-mindedly rubbing it with her apron, then using her palm to brush dust from the table top before replacing the book.

"Be glad you don't have any grown boys," Miss Maisie said in low monotones. "Just be glad that youngun's still in didies. . . . Lord knows, though, it may go on till after our time is up."

Emma didn't answer, and Genny watched Crippy as he foolishly pecked at the black dots that were the centers of faded pink roses on the linoleum. The smooth coolness felt good to the sweat-bee stings in the bends of her knees.

She wondered whether Miss Maisie would faint if one of her boys got killed and who would be able to keep her from falling if she did.

Genny and Myrtle Lou, with Gertie Spradlin, had seen Gertie's cousin Nona faint in the Spradlin family graveyard. Gertie had reported that Cousin Nona always fainted at funerals, so they were ready and waiting when the black hearse arrived, followed by about a dozen dusty cars winding close together around a curve between cedar trees. The three of them hovered on the edge of the cemetery, beside a huge tombstone with letters they couldn't quite make out, and watched as the drivers nosed their cars toward the ditches on both sides of the road. Then all the people spilled out and picked their way toward the pile of red dirt under a green tent. After Gertie told them that Cousin Nona was the one with high wedge heels, Genny fastened her eyes on her and the little mustached man whose arm she was clutching.

Genny could not make out the preacher's words, but she already knew that in the big shiny box lay Gertie's second cousin, named Pauline, and she had heard the grownups say that she was only seventeen, the prettiest and smartest of the whole bunch, and what a pity she had to go and get TB. Genny moved restively as the words droned on, and it began to seem that Cousin Nona was not going to faint at all.

Then, in a moment when there was no sound except that of a mocking bird in the weeping willow in the center of the cemetery, Cousin Nona made a sound that floated clearly to the children— a kind of drawn-out "oh," and she slid forward from her chair just under the edge of the tent. While the man with the mustache and some of the ladies bent over her, Genny suddenly wanted to find her mother and be near her. The skirt of her yellow dotted-swiss dress caught on the limb of a hawthorn bush and tore as she hurried away from Myrtle Lou and Gertie, who had gone back to try to make out the letters on the gray marker.

Lying on the floor near her brother and thinking of Cousin Nona and young dead Pauline, Genny decided that she would never faint, no matter what, but she would be sorry if one of the boys was brought back home in a casket. It would be very sad.

Miss Maisie cleared her throat and said, "If it goes on long enough, all the men'll have to go. President Roosevelt didn't want to take the farmers, leastways them with younguns, but now. . . ."

Genny was startled by her mother's addressing her sharply. "Genny Lee, take that dratted bird out of this house, hear me? All of us are going to be crawling with fleas and lice and Lord knows what all."

From his nest in the brown box, Budge whined and opened his eyelids halfway, then turned over on his stomach and began to breathe heavily again.

Genny reached for the bird and, hugging him protectively, walked through the dining room-kitchen and onto the back stoop, her back held straight and stiff to express the righteous indignation she was feeling. She sat on the gray, scratchy plank and let her pet loose to nibble at the scraps which Kaiser Bill had overlooked or rejected at noon.

She did not believe that Crippy had fleas. Since she had found him fluttering around among the rafters upstairs, she had watered him and ground corn to feed him, and she had brushed his feathers until they shone. He was all her very own, for when they heard him swishing and thumping over their heads, Myrtle Lou had screamed and half run, half fallen down the steps to the front room.

At first Genny had some reservations too, for they always pretended Great-Granny James's haint lived up there in the attic where her clothes were tied up with baling wire and suspended from a rafter to keep them away from mice. When the slightest breeze blew through the room, the gray bundle moved and swayed, and a loose sleeve seemed to beckon the children to doom. They would scream, "Granny James's haint is after us," and tumble over each other as they escaped down the steps and collapsed on the floor below, giggling and hiccupping until they were breathless.

But that time Genny had caught a glimpse of the crippled bird, and, ignoring the old rags, she had tiptoed and stretched to swoop it into her arms just as it was knocking itself against a window in a futile attempt to get out.

When she named him, he truly became her own, and she secretly planned tricks which she would teach him to perform once he was completely healed and tamed.

Now as she sat crouched on the step with her chin resting on her arms, which lay crossed on her knees, she envisioned triumphant scenes they would enact together when school started in August. By then he would readily obey her every bidding; as the sun soaked into her back and she sleepily watched Crippy Crow through half-closed lids, she pictured herself putting her name on a completed assignment and watching her classmates' astonishment as the bird took a corner in his beak and deposited the paper in the wire basket on Miss Mollie's desk. Or when Miss Mollie was working with another group, he could take a note across to Gertie and wait while she composed an answer.

She was very near to sleep, drenched in peaceful warmth, vaguely aware of the voices occasionally breaking heavy silence back in the living room. She thought she heard Budge waking up and told herself that she would go inside in a minute and bring him outside to play with her and Crippy.

Suddenly there was one loud squawk, a thud, and then, even as she looked in horror, silence. There, by the trunk of the cedar tree, where the grass didn't grow, was Crippy Crow, flat and still, just a black spot on the reddish-brown dirt. Kaiser Bill was standing nearby gnawing on a piece of dry cornbread. Then he glanced at Genny and limped on his three legs toward the spring branch for a drink of water.

With one stifled cry Genny leaped up and ran to the spot where her bird lay. When she picked him up and laid him in both palms, his head fell limply over and dangled there. The warm wad of feathers felt, already, like a *thing* that had never been alive. At that moment she did not even hate Kaiser Bill. That would have to wait. Now she just wanted Crippy not be dead.

"Please, little Crippy, breathe a little. You *can*, just try. Please, *please*, don't be *dead*."

She fell down flat on the naked ground with the tiny body touching one of her wet cheeks. But most of the tears wouldn't come out; they just stayed inside her and seemed to grow and swell there. All she could do was shake and shake. Part of her mind thought of President Roosevelt; and she pictured Sambo and Junior, across the waters, making Miss Maisie be worried to death. Her hand stroked the smooth feathers that would not move. At last, as if she were outside herself, another person entirely, she heard herself begin to cry aloud, and she bleakly wondered if she would ever be able to stop crying.

The Hawk

"When you reckon Katie'll start sewin' skirts on the little waists she makes her youngun wear?"

Aunt Widelia thought she was speaking in a low voice solely for the ears of her daughter, Nona, who sat close beside her in a high-backed rocker. But it was Aunt Widelia's deafness that made the words seem low to her, and Katie, catching every hurtful syllable as clearly as if the few feet of mostly brown yard were not between them, turned red and tried to hide her face by bending down and picking up little Mandy from a scraggly patch of grass where she had been playing contentedly. She folded her arms around the baby's pudgy legs to cover their nakedness.

Right then she decided, "If a long dress will keep 'em from makin' fun, I'll stitch her one that drags the ground. They can talk about me all they please, but little Mandy is going to be raised as nice as any of their precious younguns."

Cousin Nona, flustered, was trying to stop her ma before she "whispered" worse remarks. "Get up, Mama, and I'll move your chair to a shadier spot," she hollered close to the old woman's ear. "The sun's startin' to sift through the leaves on you."

Aunt Widelia finally understood and laboriously hoisted her large body from the rocker, balancing herself with a hard grip on Cousin Nona's forearm. After a good deal of shifting and stumbling and shouting back and forth, she was reseated in a spot protected from the mid-afternoon sun. Satisfied when she was reperched and able to breathe again without panting, she helped herself to a generous dip of snuff from the tin can her daughter handed to her.

Katie had seen enough of Hub's kin in the two years since she married him and moved to his family's home on Marah Creek, but she didn't feel on friendly terms with many of them. They didn't mind letting her know that Hub hadn't done to suit them by marrying her, a rough-handed field worker from an "ordinary" share-cropper family.

So while Aunt Widelia settled back in her chair and Cousin Nona and Miss Maisie, Hub's mama, talked on and on in their droning summertime tone, Katie sat holding her baby, fanning the flies away, slowly, methodically, not moving her arm above her wrist.

She thought how things hadn't turned out to be the way she had expected. She didn't work in the tobacco patch anymore from Monday to Friday, as she grew up doing in the various fields to which her father dragged his family. When she did try to help Hub get caught up during the busy seasons, dreaming of times when they might have something of their own, separate, the women looked down on her and said things from between thin stretched lips about wives that made mules of themselves for nothing.

And she knew well that they said things about her being plain—"ugly as a mudfence." Her own father used to say, "Katie's not much to look at, but when it comes to jumpin' about, she's a reg'lar shuck in the wind." When she had asked her mother about some way to fade her freckles, she was given only the assurance that those blemishes "wouldn't show on a galloping horse."

But a world of hope and color and joy that throbbed without reason was born inside her as she emerged into adulthood. More and more she retreated into it, and her visits were like a numbing cold drink from an everlasting spring. Then she could almost believe in her own worth and beauty. When she saw that Hub paid attention to her and she read in his looks that he meant to have her, she almost smothered in anticipation of the difference that she would finally know. But when she was in her own home, with Hub and then Mandy, she didn't feel pretty or important, after all, and she was embarrassed to think how foolish her expectations had been. Hub didn't say anything about her freckles or her big knuckles, and he didn't laugh with his relatives at the "funny ways" she had of talking; he just didn't say much of anything to her at all.

He sat now with the other menfolks, under the big maple at the corner of the yard. They leaned back on their heels, hunkered down, whittling shavings onto the ground, or just studying grass blades, talking and waiting for the long hours of Sunday evening to drag by so feeding time would come and make them feel natural again. Sometimes they laughed, loud as if they weren't really amused. They threw their heads back and laughed in unison; then Mr. Will Ed, Hub's pa, always added a big "Aw, Lawdy" at the end. It seemed to Katie that they were most often laughing at something Hub had said, and she longed to know what it was, wondered whether she would think it was funny. She pretended, in her browsing mind, that he would tell her, later, after the others had gone home, and then the two of them would laugh together, quietly as after a secret shared, so that Miss Maisie and Mr. Will Ed, in the front bedroom, wouldn't have any idea. But she knew it wouldn't happen. Not since he was courting her had he tried to make her laugh. He would keep on until she laughed herself into a spell of hiccups, and then, he would slap his thighs and roar. If she asked him tonight about what had been said, he would act as if he didn't hear her question, or else he would say, "Gollee, Katie, how'd you expect me to remember ever' little thing?"

The air was hot and heavy, and the sky was so blue and the hovering leaves so green that Katie's eyes burned. Some bees were buzzing about a bed of four-o-clocks and petunias over by the front steps, and the sound wove a sleepy tune that blended with the lazy talk and the laughter and an occasional creak of Aunt Widelia's chair as she leaned forward to spit or to take a fresh dip of snuff. Katie felt her hold on little Mandy loosen; her head nodded and jerked. Sunday afternoons were tedious, she thought, and she wished the cows would come down to the branch and bawl a reminder to the visitors that milking time wasn't far off and they ought to be getting about their business.

It was then that she heard the hawk. Her eyes widened, no trace of drowsiness now, and her back straightened to attention at the sound of the mocking, pleading call that aimed to be a song sweet enough to lure her baby chicks from the mama hen and into the tall weeds. Katie scanned the tree tops till she spied him, a black bump on a pencil-thin limb near the top of an old sycamore tree, just where the road curved to cross the creek.

At first unable to move, she watched him crouching there, and in her mind she saw the soft little balls chirping beside the mother hen, or gently rocking themselves, with eyes shut, soaking up the sun in a trance of ignorant bliss. Suddenly she was as consumed by hatred for that hawk as if he were a person capable of despising her in return and getting joy out of planning her hurt. She stood, holding Mandy on her left hip, and extended her free arm to its full length to point accusingly at the distant bird.

"I'll make you think 'chickee,' you dratted hateful thing!" she shouted. "Settin' up there doin' nothing' but wait for me to grind corn and fatten up your dinner for you!"

Hub's mama and Cousin Nona hushed their talk and stared at Katie with open mouths, surprised that she was awake, much less capable of making so much commotion right in the middle of a peaceful, decent Sunday evening. Aunt Widelia let a dip of snuff hover halfway between the can and her lip to ask Cousin Nona what on earth was the matter.

"Nothing, Mama. Just a hawk."

"A what?"

"A hawk. A hawk. Katie seen a hawk, and she's actin' like it's the first 'un she ever laid eyes on."

"Hub, that hawk'll yank ever' chicken I've got right out from under my nose, after all the care I've give 'em. Go grab the shotgun, quick!"

She kept her eyes on the hawk, even as she called to her husband, as if her gaze could pin him to the limb, prevent him from swooping down with his sharp claws and his tearing beak.

Hub spoke slowly, still whittling. "Get it yourself; you know where it's at. Why'd I be shootin' that old hawk? That black devil's my buddy. He's fixin' to save me 'bout a wagon load of nubbins. Ain't that right, fellers?"

Then they all laughed, and Mr. Will Ed said his "Aw, Lawdy." Katie heard Hub's mama clear her throat, loud, in a pleased way, and she could clearly see, without looking around, Cousin Nona trying to keep from showing her teeth, but secretly grinning all the same.

Katie felt a hot wave gush over her face and ears, and she knew what must be done. She set Mandy down on the grass and ran onto the shallow porch and into the long hall that cut the house in two. She flung open the door of the "front room" and entered its dankness without noticing the unpleasantness of stale air and darkness which always assailed her. She was familiar with the heavy furniture that lurked in shadows, though the room was rarely opened except for funerals or, sometimes, when the preacher made a call.

The shotgun was cold when she lifted it from its dark corner beside the tall chifforobe. The alien metal seemed at the same time to freeze and burn her trembling hand. She laid it gently on the floor, mistrusting the violence it represented, and fumbled in the top drawer for a shell. She fingered it cautiously, as if it might explode at her touch. All the while she was thinking of Hub and Cousin Nona and the others out there laughing as if she was nobody, unconcerned about the little lives that were being threatened. And all the time she was afraid the hawk would fly away before she could get back outside and aim.

But it was still there all right, a hateful black speck like a small puncture in the blue sky. She stung under a full barrage of fun-making eyes, and she concentrated on ignoring them. She tried to keep her arm steady and aim as she had seen Hub do when he allowed her to go squirrel-hunting with him, during the exciting days when they were going together. The sound was a surprise in the still Sunday air, even though she had finally willed her own finger to pull the trigger. She could not guess whether the sound simply warned him he'd better be moving, postponing for the moment the infliction of evil. He fluttered on the end of his thin limb and then slowly flew toward the distance, like a wavy pencil-mark getting dimmer and dimmer until it faded out before her straining eyes.

In the side yard the mother hen was clucking and calling to her babies in a begging, worried tone, and peeping chickens came running from under hollyhocks and rosebushes, as if they sensed that they had just had a narrow escape.

At that moment Katie was snatched back to reality by the frantic yells of little Mandy.

"Pore bit of a youngun," said Miss Maisie. "You scared her to death with that gun. Come on, Dumplin'. Granny'll take you." In Miss Maisie's fat lap the baby continued to scream, tears mixing with grass stains she had smeared from her hands to her flushed cheeks.

Katie quickly leaned the gun against the trunk of a shade tree, forgetful of everything except her frightened baby. She snatched her up and held her close, kissing her wet face over and over.

"Did Mama scare her baby? Mama didn't mean to, and she won't do it again. Mama won't shoot the mean old gun again. Hush, sweet baby." She sat down and joggled the straight chair back and forth until the steady bump-bump lulled Mandy to sleep and peace.

Aunt Widelia rocked back and forth and mumbled on and on about hawks and chickens and varmints and chickens. "Gusta ain't got but five chicks left out of two settin's she took off the nest this spring," she marveled for her own benefit.

"That was last year, Mama," Cousin Nona corrected. Then to Miss Maisie: "Did you hear that Ada Belle come home yesterday?"

Katie held Mandy closer and kept rocking, but her heart thumped and fluttered in her ears as if she had been hoeing hard in the hot sun. She remembered Miss Gusta's daughter Ada Belle, big-eyed and plump, with flesh pones that made her skin-tight dress shimmer as she walked with a twist. She remembered the painted lines that had replaced pulled-out eyebrows and the way they emphasized her hard look as she glared at Katie, hating her from the start for taking Hub away from her. That was two years ago, at the Baptist Church where Hub had taken her, and as they walked into the half-filled assembly, Ada Belle had glanced around and seen them; then she had nudged the girl beside her, and their backs both shook with giggles. There hadn't been any fun in her eyes, though; Katie read in them a naked hatred. She had no doubt that Ada Belle had it in for her from the start.

"I saw her at church this morning," Cousin Nona went on, showing by her tone that she knew she had an interested audience now. "Struttin' like a peacock, too" she added, but showing that she meant it as a compliment. "I reckon she must have an awful good job up there in Detroit, the way she dresses like the president's wife and all. And she's always sendin' Miss Gusta a sachet or fancy pillow top or such."

"Takin' her vacation, I reckon," Miss Maisie said. Then she sighed long and hard. "Law mercy, that child always treated me like I was a second mammy to her, and that's the truth. Little did I dream—them two a-eatin' each other up since they were little bitty rascals, and goin' to BYPU together every Sunday night of the world, and her comin' by and offerin' to tote Hub a fresh jug of water to the field, and then standin' in the fence row to watch him clear to the end of a furrow. Well, mark my words, they's generally something bad comes of goin' against what was meant to be."

Katie's face felt hot, and the tips of her fingers were cold as ice, as though they had been held in the spring branch for the longest time. Why don't they hush up, she thought, almost prayed, talking this way like I couldn't understand or like they don't care anyhow. She was glad baby Mandy was still too young to understand and be hurt too.

Somehow Aunt Widelia had caught the drift of this conversation, and with a kind of wicked glint in her eyes she cleared her mouth by spitting energetically between two fingers, and then she called over to Katie. "Say, Katie, what would you do should you catch Hub and Ada Belle honeying around together, like in the old times?"

Now she could feel Miss Maisie and Cousin Nona eying her too, all curiosity. She wouldn't have answered, except that she knew Aunt Widelia would keep on and get louder until she received a response. Because of the flutter of her heart and the sick, uneasy knot lying in the top of her stomach, her tongue let loose words her own ears were astounded to hear.

"I reckon I might pull me two people bald-headed."

Aunt Widelia heard the first time. "Well, I do know!" she declared, delighted. She threw back her head till it popped against the wood slats and kept making rusty puffs of laughter. Then she twisted sidewise in her chair.

"Did you hear that, John Herbert?"

The men looked up. "What's that, Aunt Deley?" Hub asked.

"Katie allows she might pull you and Ada Belle plumb bald-headed."

For a long moment the air took on an extra heaviness, like the quiet period after a thunderclap when you're trying to be ready for the next one so as not to jump. Katie kept her eyes lowered upon the sleeping child in her lap, but she did not need to look to see the red flush darken over Hub's already wind-burned face and neck and turn to pink the white rim left by a recent haircut. She knew, without looking, the taut line around his mouth which hardened when he became angry. His answer was flung at her, not at all at Aunt Widelia.

"If there's any hair-pullin' to be done, I 'magine I'll be the one doin' the yankin'," he said.

There was another moment of silence while his words, heavy with anger and spite, churned in the air between the men and the women. Then Mr. Will Ed laughed, and that caused all the others to laugh, loud, except for Cousin Nona, whose mirth showed only in her eyes and her shoulders. Little Mandy whimpered and raised her head, and Katie patted her back, under the loose cotton shift, until she sank again into sleep.

"He's mad," she thought. "Mad as old Hector, but he'll get over it."

And "He'll get over it," she repeated to herself at sundown as she milked the cows in their darkened stalls, smelling the wild onions on their breath and hearing only the sounds of their methodical chewing and the changing tones of milk squirting on metal and then into filling buckets. Above her, in the loft, Hub's feet moved with angry clumps and sent clouds of hay dust down through wide cracks upon her head.

Again as they lay in bed, still separated by an alienating silence, she told herself with decreasing confidence that Ada Belle could do her no harm now—could do nothing to endanger the future of her baby. She reached her hand to the moveless form of the sleeping child, lying on her stomach in the baby bed pulled up to touch the side of the double bed. Her fingers discovered a smooth leg, cooled already by the damp night air. Her ears heard the insistent cry of whippoorwills, coming to her sometimes as sad, sometimes vindictive, and the creek slopping around protruding roots, and the death message of a screech owl from somewhere across the creek. From Hub's side of the bed, where she knew he was lying awake, she could feel, like heat waves rising from a sun-baked August field, anger—and hatred?

"He'll get over it," she repeated to herself until it sounded like a prayer. "I'll make it come out all right for us, Mandy," she promised silently, and then she fell into a dream-haunted sleep with her hand still dangling onto the other bed.

Next morning, after breakfast and milking were accomplished in silence, he announced in a sullen voice that he was going to walk over to the pike and catch a ride into Shiloh. He had to have some axle grease, he volunteered, though Katie would not have dared ask him for a reason. Wordlessly she laid out clean overalls and shirt and socks, and she gave an extra shine to his good slippers with the tail of her dress. Leaving him still changing clothes, she went about building a fire around the kettle in the back yard and filling it, bucket by bucket, with water from the spring.

Later, when sheets and towels were flapping in the wind and a tubful of colored clothes had been put to soak, she decided to take a bucket of dry ashes back to the truck-patch to sprinkle around the cucumber vines. Miss Maisie said that was a sure way to run destructive hard-backed bugs clear out of the field. She lifted Mandy from her pallet under the squatty cherry tree, held her a-straddle her left hip, and carried the heavy bucket in her right hand. She started to cross the creek and take the shorter path that wound through the woods and up to the cleared land. On second thought, the extra steps down the creek seemed more desirable than the steep climb with her heavy double load.

The path along the creek was soft and spongy where it was covered with several years' droppings of pine needles. Now and then a bullfrog croaked or plopped into the water so close by her that she jumped. As she walked, she stepped around tall crawfish towers, covered over in anticipation of drought, or so the old people said.

Walking along like the ghost of an Indian squaw wandering still in some forgotten age, Katie admitted to herself that she had secretly intended to come this way from the start, for the path she was following wound past Miss Gusta's old house, and she was pulled, with a power too strong to be denied, in the direction that might allow her to lay eyes on Ada Belle. The path crossed the shallow creek just before reaching the dilapidated gray frame house, and Katie crossed carefully on flat limestone slabs, tightening her hold on Mandy. Another turn of the path and she would be able to see straight onto the front porch; but nobody would be able to see her because tall bushes lined the opposite side of the creek. Straightaway she heard voices coming from the porch.

"Prob'ly Miss Gusta and Ada Bell a-hullin' beans or something," she thought.

She had not known that she was half holding her breath in fear, but when she rounded the curve and saw the two people on the porch, she suddenly knew that this was what her feet had been rushing her to see, what she didn't want to see, dreaded to see—but had to see because it was there. She stopped still, holding Mandy and the bucket, not even thinking to set the bucket on the ground, only thinking that for some reason she must look and look at the scene that put a physical ache in her chest where her heart cowered.

They were sitting near the end of the porch, close together in the old swing that always hung there, even in winter when no one would think of sitting in it. The end of the porch was screened by morning-glory vines so that the two were sitting in shade with only small puddles of morning sun finding them where they were. One bit of butter-yellow light fell on Ada Belle's hair, and Katie could tell, even from that distance, that it was dyed. She had on a pink Sunday-ish dress, it looked to be pongee, with a low neck and a skirt too short to cover her crossed knees even if she had wanted it to. Hub sat beside her in his clean overalls that were shiny and smooth from Katie's starching and ironing in her hot kitchen. He had an arm across the back of the swing, and he wasn't sulled, not anymore. They were laughing and talking—laughing loud and talking low—and Katie wondered if she wished she could hear their words.

Ada Belle flounced about in the swing as she giggled, and the old chains squeaked rustily. Then one of Ada Belle's shoes fell off. It was wedge-heeled, very high and without a back. She squealed when it fell to the plank floor, and Hub bent over to pick it up. As he did, Ada Belle bent too and bit him on the neck, her giggle turning to a laugh deep down in her throat, and Hub forgot all about the shoe. From the other side of the creek all Katie could hear was the groaning and squeaking of the swing.

She could still hear it as she walked back up the path, not toward the field but the way she had come. Her feet, without the help of her mind, felt their way around roots and stobs. She bent to protect Mandy's face from low-hanging branches, but she was seeing only what she had seen and hearing what she had heard. Part of her mind was surprised that she was so calm, that she could go on walking and thinking as if the world hadn't the same as come to an end for her.

She foresaw the years stretching ahead of her and Mandy as if she were a cold stranger contemplating somebody else's sad fate. It was like the times when as a child she had gone to town, down five miles of dusty road; and her eyes would search and search for black spots cast by trees or a cloud that might soon shelter her for a moment from the scorching sun. And when no spots could be seen, the road stretched on forever in hot dustiness; then Katie could not imagine ever reaching town, finding the end of the tiresome road, and being rested and cooled again in her whole life. She felt that way now, with a despair that made her numb.

Reaching the house, thinking fleetingly how glad she was that Hub's parents were off on one of their visits with kinfolks, she put down the bucket and set the baby back on her pallet, handing her a string of spools to pacify her for a while. Then she entered the house and went once more into the cool, unused room with its smell of funerals and faded flowers and forgotten old books. Without glancing around or hesitating, she hurried to the corner where the shotgun had been put back in its place. Taking a shell from the drawer, she loaded the gun, feeling the merest tremor at the touch and at the thought of what it would help her to do. For a moment she stood, thinking different ways, and then she took another shell and dropped it into her apron pocket. She started and caught her breath when she glimpsed herself, a furtive stranger, in the fuzzy gray depths of the chifforobe mirror. Closing the door quietly, she continued down the hall to the back of the house and then to the path.

"Little Mandy, don't miss me, please, just for a few minutes," she whispered.

She carried the gun with both hands, holding it in front of her and away from her body. The black-cold of the barrel and the slippery chill of polished wood burned into her palms. As the cold metal of Hub's car door had burned into her back, that night, after church, when they parked at Spout Spring, where the weeping willow reaches to the ground; and afterwards, when the circle of Hub's arm burned through her flesh and left a sting that she could still feel later, when she lay in her own bed and wondered at the certainty that had come to her—that he meant to marry her.

She had not gone up the path very far when she heard Mandy set up a loud scream. "Oh, Lord," Katie said aloud, and her heart turned wildly in her breast and began to feel again after numbness, hurting like a foot waking up. She spun around and began to run back, regardless of the limbs that whipped her face. She held the gun carelessly, dangling it beside her like a dead stick.

"Mama's coming, Baby! Oh, Lord, if she should be hurt!"

Mandy continued to scream as Katie reached the pallet. She had crawled to the edge of the spread quilt and somehow turned over the bucket of ashes which Katie had left in the grass. Her face and arms were streaked with wet ashes and tears. Katie laid the gun in the grass and sat flat on the ground, holding the baby and rocking back and forth and moaning.

"Oh, my baby, what's goin' to become of us? What are we goin' to do in this world? Oh, Lord, Lord, Lord, Lord."

An old dominecker hen and her chickens found the pile of spilled ashes and busily began to scratch up smoky clouds. The discarded gun glinted blackly in the mellow sunlight, and the chickens pecked mindlessly at the metal, while the hen clucked deep in her throat to call them to their quest for food.

Final Payment

*C*ornelia was dead at last. Now it was hard to imagine her as young and vibrant or any other way than she was right now, lying in a shining gray casket in her own dim parlor, her lavender crepe dress soaking up the shadows that hungrily enveloped the still, brief form and made soft purple concaves about her closed eyes. She was too unreal to elicit grief; only now and then those present responded with an attempt at decent silence between forgetful outbursts that brought into the room snatches from the energetic surges that comprised life and therefore resented interstices breaking its flow.

Dozens of cousins and self-proclaimed kinsfolk of vague connections flocked to the house on the day after her death and even more on the next, several of them laying early claim to beds in the four upstairs rooms and making plans for staying until after the funeral. Others who lived beyond the immediate neighborhood stayed with friends or relatives overnight, reconvening at the Moore home early on the morning of the funeral. Cornelia's two nieces, children of Lizzie, went directly to the little house which the Reverend W. E. Moore, Cornelia's husband, had built in the back yard for her sisters. The sole remaining White sister, Parthenia, now lived there alone. She welcomed the girls, themselves well on the way to becoming spinsters after the fashion of all the White females except Lizzie and, of course, Cornelia. Parthenia was a faded relic of a colorful day when she and her sisters were expected and welcome additions to all the playparties and barbecues for miles around.

For many years, all who knew Cornelia had held to the general opinion that she was a peculiar and cold woman; and, having reached this conclusion, they ceased making any overtures and mostly ignored her, at the same time feeling sorry for Brother Moore, whose warmth and geniality were universally recognized and constantly praised. They speculated as to the reasons a talented and outgoing minister and citizen like him could have had for allying himself with such a woman as Cornelia.

Now that she was dead, neighbors and kinspeople hurried to the side of the widower, still spry and active at seventy-four. They found him, on the day of the funeral, wandering under the cedars in the front yard, tall and wiry like the trees. He was, as always, immaculate in a black suit and white shirt, over which his long beard floated like fluffed cotton. He embraced all who approached him with offers of sympathy, and then he stood holding each proffered hand between his own two hands, shaping words of grief and loss and acceptance into majestic phrases that would have sounded appropriate under great carved beams, echoing against panes of intricately designed stained glass.

Many of the visitants recalled images from past years of Brother Moore and his wife sitting stiffly side by side in the buggy that he always kept in prime condition, gliding swiftly toward some religious assembly or other without any evidence of feeling ruts or holes. Others found, forgotten under piles of stored mental pictures, an image of Brother Moore and Miss Cornelia sitting on their shady front porch on a long summer afternoon as if perpetually waiting for company to drive down the narrow gravel road and hitch their horses to one of the posts at the side of the white weatherboard house. In Brother Moore's presence, one succumbed to the magic of his practiced voice and temporarily forgot those later years when Miss Cornelia rarely came out of the rambling house, never stepped her foot outside the yard to visit a neighbor or go to church or a brush arbor meeting with her husband. In fact, nearly everyone on hand to witness her burial had, at most, one or two remembrances of a much younger Cornelia Moore, and even these pictures had faded to a blur until she could have been any one of the dozens of brown shadows secured between the pages of a family album.

Ladies in silks and crepes of subdued colors moved to and fro in the big square room where Cornelia's body lay. They whispered behind cupped hands, mumbling low, with their heads held so close together that sometimes their hat brims touched. Occasionally a cluster of them tiptoed into the adjoining dining room, removed their gloves, and helped themselves to crumbly slices of cake and tiny biscuits filled with slivered ham. They perched on edges of straight-back chairs, their own backs held rigid by corsets and, even more, by a sense of propriety that each encouraged in the other. They sipped tea and nibbled daintily as they pooled their memories of Cornelia, bent on determining which of them had been the last to glimpse her outside the house, or inside it, for that matter.

Mrs. Sibbie Shelton knew for certain that she had had her own last view of Cornelia upon the occasion of another funeral right there in that same identical parlor. That time Cornelia had sat in one of the parlor chairs beside other family members, as still and silent as she was now. That funeral had been for her and Brother Moore's own son, James Robert, who lay in a casket draped with a flag whose bright slashes of color cut the grayness of the room like pain.

"I'll never forget, if I live to be a hundred," said Mrs. Shelton, "how that woman sat there, all the way through Brother Moore's precious words, acting like the whole affair was no more to her than a fly buzzing. Less. Never shed a solitary tear the whole time, not even when the telegram came, so I heard."

"I can vouch for that, Sibbie," put in Miss Dollie Eller eagerly. "I'm the one that brought the news out from town. It was 1918; it doesn't seem possible I've had my little car seven years, but it was new then, and Mr. Baldwin over at the Telegraph Office in the hotel saw me going in the Mercantile, so he asked me would I bring this message out to the Moores."

"And she didn't cry even at *that?*" asked Miss Lucy Spann in disbelief.

"I'm coming to it, Lucy. When I drove up at the front gate, several of those black grandyounguns of Froney that still lives in the cabin by the creek were playing round by the fence. Young Dothan, that's their daddy, was right out yonder where the men are standing, shoeing Brother Moore's saddle horse. Well, I knew Dothan was crazy about J.R., back when they were both little, so I told him the news. And would you believe those little fuzzy-headed scamps heard me and ran ahead to holler it to J.R.'s wife!"

"Oh, Dollie," the ladies chorused in horror.

"Yes. She was up in that low loft over the tool shed sorting out fruit jars, and when she heard the racket, she came over and leaned out the window to see what was going on. 'Miss Helen, yo' man's daid,' they hollered, jumping up and down like the dirt was scorching their bare feet. And right then, without a word, she leaped through that window and kind of turned a tumbleset before she lay right still and flat on the ground. I tell you, my heart stopped beating."

"Wasn't she . . . ," somebody began.

"I thought for certain I was going to have to tend to a birthing then and there. I was bending over Helen considering what to do when my eye caught some movement, and I looked up and saw Cornelia standing there with both hands on the banister, just looking at us." Miss Dollie glanced over toward the coffin as if half expecting some corroborative statement.

"Did she faint?" asked one of the ladies.

"*Faint?* I reckon not. She just looked at Helen, and she looked at me, and then she just peered up through the elm branches out there, straight up, up at the patch of sky—y'all know how she could stick that sharp chin into the air and stretch her mouth—and then she just stood there, I tell you, with her face looking like she had somehow slipped off and left her body standing there empty. Seemed like the news I brought was something somebody had drug up from a ragged old paper in the attic that she had already read a thousand times—that's how interested she looked to be."

"Probably the bit of a baby broke the ice, though," guessed Miss Sibbie.

"That was two weeks after the funeral," said Miss Dollie, "but I heard it just made matters worse. Froney told Sophy that does my ironing that Cornelia couldn't stand the sight of that precious orphan grandson, in fact, purely fell apart after he got a little older and took to running around in his shirttail under everybody's foot. Helen started leaving him back there with his Aunt Parthy a good deal of the time. Then finally she just packed up and moved her and him to Pennsylvania, where her people are. She must have started him to school up there by now. You don't see them here for this funeral, notice. A woman that wouldn't be touched by her own dead son's body is *cold*, mark my words!"

The ladies took their saucers to the kitchen and trailed back to the parlor to relocate themselves on sofas and chairs arranged close together around the wall and to chat in undertones with recent comers.

One lady sitting near a table by the front door picked up a worn black leather book and began to thumb through its yellowed pages. Black spidery writing covered the sheets on both sides. She punched the lady next to her and showed her that these were names of couples at whose weddings the Reverend Moore had officiated.

"There's Frank and me!" exclaimed the lady, more loudly than she was aware, making everybody stop talking for a moment and look curiously in her direction.

"Mercy, that was so long ago the sheet's crumbling, you might know," she chuckled, passing the book along to someone who was holding out her hand for it. "We have a picture took right over there in front of that mantel. Law, my sleeves practically took up the whole space, so much material in them back then. The White sisters, still hanging there, they're in it dim. Cornelia stood up with me, you know."

"Was she . . . strange, then?" a pink-faced lady asked, leaning over so far to hear that her ample bosoms almost overbalanced her.

"Strange? No . . . o, I wouldn't say that. Seems like they'd lost a baby the winter before, had the croup or measles or something. So she was probably sad, but real nice and all like you'd expect Brother Moore's wife to be."

"The Lord giveth and the Lord taketh away," intoned a lady sunk down into a corner of the sofa. Everybody silently accepted this truth.

"And blessed be the Name," finally completed an old lady peering from behind a veil with tiny daisies embroidered on it. "You don't expect to raise all your children." Then everyone sank into her own thoughts for a long while, and the voices of the men outside and the droning of dryflies floated in through open doors and windows.

"Y'all probably have heard Brother Moore's sermon on 'Behold the goodness and the severity of God,'" said Miss Dollie. "It's one of his best, and they're all good. He can hit the nail right on the head."

There was unanimous agreement, as shown by nods and brief verbal affirmations.

"They did have other children, didn't they? You mentioned a John Robert?" This was from a lady who had just arrived from one of Brother Moore's churches in Houston County.

"*James* Robert," corrected Miss Sibbie, whose brother had been married to Brother Moore's late sister, which practically made her a member of the family, though she had been living in Mississippi for several years and had somewhat lost touch.

"He was there at our wedding I was telling you about," exclaimed the lady by the door. "I can just see him peeping from behind a big chair in that corner with his blue eyes as big and round as saucers and looking just like his papa's. And the precious thing, now that I remember, was cutting teeth, and his slobber was all over his front, soaking wet. And Cornelia about ready to have another one—I didn't mention that."

"Where's *it?*" someone broke in. "The baby she was about to have, I mean."

"Something happened to him," Miss Dollie began.

"Drowned," said Miss Sibbie, glad that they were back to something she knew about. "It was awful, even I couldn't find out much about it. But Cornelia just about went crazy for awhile—I know that." She shook her head and dealt privately with memories that were too vague or too painful to share.

"A shame," came a voice. "We just have to accept. It's our sacred duty." They all nodded and then shook their heads in silence.

Cornelia's sister Parthenia, who had been occupied for most of the morning at her own little house in the back yard, re-entered the parlor from the kitchen. She went around and accepted hugs from everyone, including those who had been there earlier when she had taken her leave. The two ladies on the sofa moved over to allow her room to sit in the middle, and several others eased their chairs a little nearer to join the conversation group.

Parthenia folded her hands on her black skirt. Her slim blue-veined hands were bare, as if *any* ring would serve as a reminder of the absence of the kind most coveted. It was rumored in the neighborhood that, back before Cornelia or any of the other Whites had moved to Yellow Creek, she had loved a fine, handsome man who had moved off to Texas and had never been heard from again. Others said it was a Confederate soldier who went away to fight and die. She would have been very young at that time, they speculated, but a certain romantic aura continued to attach itself to this White sister, making her somehow more lovable than Cornelia.

She glanced across at Cornelia's form and at the vase of huge red and white dahlias which someone had set on a stool at the foot of the coffin.

"Poor 'Nelia," she sighed. She hasn't been happy for so long. I'm glad she's seeing some peace at last."

"Yes, we all felt for her and for Brother Moore too," said Miss Dollie. "And you too, dear. Tell us, was it hard for her at the end?"

"Oh, no, at least, we don't know exactly what happened. You know, she never went out of the house for years—not even downstairs except for necessities. Well, you all remember how it stormed day before yesterday, a little before sunset?"

"Talk about close lightning! I reckon I do remember!" said one lady while the others nodded and waited.

"Well, I let my windows down when it started looking dark and heavy, and then I crossed over here to see to the ones in this house. About the time I finished, the bottom fell out—and thunder so loud the furniture rattled. So I just piddled around in here till it let up. I guess it was almost dark when I started back across the yard, and I heard little old Snooks barking down toward the creek. First thing I thought was he went with Eb—Brother Moore—that morning; anyway, I hadn't seen him in the house. Then I thought what if Brother Moore's horse had slipped on the slick limestones down by the creek. You know how it is when those dark thoughts set in to gnaw."

"Law, yes. You can just imagine anything. Terrible!" One lady said it, and they all agreed, talking at once.

"So I picked my way through the muddy weeds, holding my skirt up, and when I got nearly to the creek, I couldn't believe my eyes, for there she was, lying face down in the mud with her gray dress spread on the ground and Snooks barking his head off and sniffling around the edge of it—of her." She clinched her hands together as she recalled the scene.

"Well, had the lightning struck her?" Miss Sibbie asked, not knowing anymore than the others what actually happened.

"No, it wasn't that. We could've told that. As Providence would have it, Brother Moore came riding up, back from court, right after I came upon her, though it seemed an eternity, and he got down and felt her heart and pulse and all, and then he picked her up and carried her back up here to the house while I led King."

"But how did she get there? That's what I'd like to know," came from Miss Dollie, who had moved her chair closer to the sofa.

"Miss Dollie, we'll never know. I can't imagine why she went out of the house at all, much less in a storm. She was deathly afraid of storms, never came out of her room for anything while one was going on. I mean, even in her good years. It all goes back to her horse, Silver, that got struck. Sibbie, you remember that?"

Sibbie sat up straighter. "Lord, I'd all but forgot it. It was that horse your Pa willed her, and a mate to the one he left Lizzie."

"Yes, and my Plume that I rode so long and still have the sidesaddle he willed to me with her. My, we loved those horses; that's what Pa knew when he left them to us."

About that time Parthenia had to go to the door to greet Cousin Eleanor Barnes and her husband, who had just arrived from Clarksdale, come to pay their last respects to Cornelia. Parthenia walked between them, arm in arm, to stand beside the casket, and then she escorted them to the dining room door and bade them help themselves to the refreshments.

The ladies had eagerly waited, their eyes following the strangers. They moved their feet out of Parthenia's path as she reclaimed her spot on the sofa.

"Let's see. Oh. Well, it was after 'Nelia's baby drowned and she'd been real bad, but she was back at herself by then—at least, we thought she was, though she was real quiet and you could catch her looking far off at some awful sight that you couldn't see or imagine. Well, it was summer, and she had saddled up Silver to take a little ride by herself, first time since it happened. But you know how fast those afternoon clouds come up and like as not go away just as fast. So she thought she'd better wait and see. She tied Silver to the hook on the top of the gate post and walked on over to the front porch. I was in this very room reading to J.R., and when I heard her steps, I got up to take a look at the cloud. Just as I opened the screen door, she screamed and crumpled down on the porch, tearing at her hair with both hands."

"Was she struck that time?" someone asked, and all were so carried away by the excitement of the narrative that they would have believed anything.

"No," said Parthenia. "Silver was. When I looked, he was standing on his hind legs with his front hooves pawing at the sky, clouds rather, it looked like a cyclone was about to hit at any minute, and his eyes were rolled back in his head wild and piti-ful. And the sound—oh, ladies, I can't tell you how awful it was!"

"What was it?" they all wanted to know.

"Silver's scream—it sounded like a human scream, all crazy and hurt and mad as a hornet. Then he fell back with bloody foam all over his face and his four legs sticking straight up, just as stiff as those table legs."

"Terrible," shivered Miss Dollie, glancing at the nearby table legs to help her imagine it. "No wonder if Cornelia was touched in the head after that."

"Bad things *do* happen. We have to accept them," admon-ished the solemn veiled lady from over by the window.

"I've heard," said Parthenia, "that if you look straight at a lightning bolt when it's coming down that you always lose your mind, never get back to normal. I'm thankful to the Lord that I didn't come out of this house to look a second sooner than I did."

"Cooks the brain, I guess," Miss Sibbie mused. "Well, all I know is, Cornelia was never the same. Going out into that storm day before yesterday was only the last straw."

The men were setting up benches and chairs under the cedar trees in the front yard, where the funeral would be held. Some of the ladies rose, smoothed their dresses, and put on their gloves; then for some reason tiptoeing, they filed onto the front porch to secure for themselves good vantage points from which to observe the service and every nuance of Brother Moore's manner and presentation. They wanted to be where they could see and hear him clearly, for they couldn't believe it humanly possible for one to be so brave and dedicated as to conduct the funeral rites for his own wife. Others left the parlor to proceed through the kitchen and into the small back bedroom, desiring to freshen up before the funeral. Parthenia, showing them the way, met a black woman coming into the kitchen from the back porch. Seeing Parthenia and the group of ladies behind her, the woman stood still, her hand tentatively clutching the screen door latch.

"Why, Froney, bless your heart, come on in," said Parthenia. "I told young Dothan this morning that it would be fine if you came over right before the funeral time and told Miss Cornelia goodbye. Come on in this way."

Froney followed Parthenia reluctantly, hanging back at the door leading to the parlor, the whites of her frightened eyes gleaming. Parthenia reached over to pull her to her side. Froney covered her face with the bright scarf that she had draped over a navy blue dress that used to belong to Parthenia herself. Her narrow body shook under the dress, which hung limply off her shoulders. Her voice was deep and trembling.

"Miss Nelie and me, we had us a time," she said, and then she said the same words over several times. "Us two sure did have us a time."

"She thought a lot of you, Froney," assured Parthenia, checking the round gold watch that hung among the ruffles of her crisp white blouse.

"Y'all's paw said he wanted me to stay with Miss Nelie," said Froney proudly. "That's why me and young Dothan and the younguns get to live back there on the place. She knowed I'd do what I could for her."

"She always knew that, Froney," Parthenia assured her, patting her on the arm and gently pushing her in the direction of the kitchen, for it was time for the funeral to begin. But instead of letting herself be moved, Froney bent over to speak directly into Cornelia's marble face. The ladies from the bedroom came back through just in time to stand by Parthenia and share her amazement.

"Well, Miss Nelie," Froney said, "I'm sorry about them buggers. I wish I could of shot 'em for you, but I couldn't get rid of 'em any more'n you could. But don't you worry none, sweet lady. You're shut of them buggers now." She reached into the casket and laid her flat black hand over both of Cornelia's colorless ones.

"They've bothered me some too, but you've had a harder time than me. Lawd, Miss Nelie, I can see it all plain as today and hear them logs going bumpbumpbump against the bridge down there where it happened. There's me stirring away in the kittle, lifting them white things up and down in the bilin' suds, and there's you in your purty Monday dress with spriglets on it. And there's little Willie playin' around your feet like a feisty pup, pilin' up rocks or ridin' his broomstick horsie. There's you agin, asmilin' like and spreadin' purty little things that you washed separate on the bushes. Then there's that big voice that's Brother Moore callin' you inside and you smilin' and runnin' in like you used to do. There's that plague-takit little yellow butterfly that flittered around till it made little Willie follow it right through the clover field and . . . and there's me stirrin' away and gittin' all hot and steamy and swattin' sweatbees, and forgittin' everythin'."

Froney stood for a while as if in that same trance-like state that she was describing, perfectly still except for the hand that gently straightened the pale pink ruffle circling Cornelia's tiny wrist. The ladies waited breathlessly, their gloved hands clutching their purses.

"Cain't blame you for screamin' when you found him gone, Miss Nelie. And me, I thow'd that paddle windin' and run right after you toward what we's afraid to see. And there, hung on a root lookin' like one of them piles of rags that stuck there when the creek was up. . . ."

She stopped and covered up her eyes with hands that mashed hard as if to eradicate what she was seeing.

"But Miss Nelie," she almost whispered, bending lower over the casket, so that it was hard for the others to hear, "Miss Nelie, I think you're wrong and you shore skeered me to say them things about you and God and all. Me'n you couldn't he'p it. And it wasn't Brother Moore's doin' for callin' you to him. It wan't. That old creek just done its do, and them buggers plain wouldn't turn you loose. But now they has, ain't they, sweet Miss Nelie? You done outrun 'em now, that's for sure."

She removed her hands from the side of the casket and allowed herself to be steered into the kitchen. Miss Parthenia found a piece of waxed paper and wrapped some goodies for Dothan and the children. Froney accepted the package without paying any attention to it. With her free hand she wiped her scarf across her face vigorously as she crossed the backyard.

She had almost reached her cabin when she heard singing starting up in Brother Moore's front yard. The words of "Shall We Gather at the River?" floated clearly to her ears as she kicked her way among the children's playtoys and Young Dothan's tools to enter the cool darkness of her home, where she could have some peace to cry the tears that just had to be spilled out for Miss Nelie's sake.

The Long Dark Hall

The first glimpse I had of the Harpers was on a Monday morning, the fifth day of my vigil at Mercy Hospital. My step was a bit lighter as I strode down the hall toward the now familiar Intensive Care Waiting Room. A new skirt, soft and pink around my legs, was my way of celebrating the renewal of hope; my sister Erna was at last free of the breathing machine following the worst spell she had ever suffered of pneumonia, and if she continued to improve, I could see her installed in a convalescent home in a matter of days. Then I could return to my job in the local library and relax into relative normalcy. My suede heels clicked cheerfully against the tiled floor, and I had no inkling of what was about to happen or of its long-lasting impact upon my very being.

Later I speculated that those two extraordinary people might not have affected me as they did if they had appeared days earlier, while my sister's life hung in the balance. I do not deny that it is outside my nature to become involved in lives foreign to myself. Though I maintain a friendly relationship with many of the frequenters of the library who seek my help—most of them retirees, decades older than I—I have not cared to cultivate personal relationships. It is safer to keep closer ties with a few who fit into my predictable routine and demand little.

After almost a week, though, I had managed to establish something of a pattern that lent the kind of security I cherished. I was actually looking forward to settling myself cozily in the waiting room, sipping coffee and browsing through my newspaper until time for the nine o'clock visit.

As I approached the double doors, shiningly free of yesterday's smudged fingerprints, pondering the ordinary activities to which I would soon return, I didn't look straight at the two people sitting side by side, facing the door. But I knew that they were not any of those relatives of the seriously ill whose faces had become a familiar part of this setting, as expected as the vase of artificial tulips in the middle of the low coffee table or the television that never ceased its babbling from a shelf above our heads. I vaguely thought that something bad had befallen someone they cared about, something that had brought them in a rush from their homes to this place since I left the hospital on Sunday evening. I sat down a couple of chairs away from the old woman and began to arrange myself for a quiet hour of waiting.

It was always like this until near the designated hours for visiting: few people, little mingling or talking. Then, as the time approached, the long room would begin to fill, and the low hum would increase to an anxious din of raised voices and scraping chairs.

I groped in my tapestry tote bag for the morning paper. Then, in spite of myself, I glanced toward the end of the room where, with his back to me, stood the young husband who spent every night in a leather lounge chair in the corner, refusing to leave his wife, who had recently been diagnosed as having an advanced case of leukemia. I had watched him each morning, standing like that, his hands clenched on the window sill against which he leaned, staring out at a glittering skyline he likely was not seeing. I turned away and unfolded the *Herald*, willing the hurt to go away, the tightness to let go of my throat; for the sympathy that fluttered within me was disconcerting, uncomfortable.

— 42 —

Bringing my glance nearer, I began to focus on the new couple. What I had at first thought, with the small portion of my mind that took note, was that it was an old man and woman huddled together in their shared despair, facing the door in the silence of dread. I tried to eye them unobtrusively as I rummaged in my bag for my change purse, getting ready for the two gray-haired ladies in peach-toned uniforms to roll in their carts stocked with fragrant coffee and doughnuts. I idly wondered if that little couple would revive enough to partake of something, but they ignored all the bustle and remained as immobile as statues.

I limited my staring to my acute peripheral vision, for I certainly had no wish to become involved and maybe even drawn into a depressing conversation with strangers. The woman was obviously large, for she fitted snugly into her chair; short, stubby legs in wrinkled cotton stockings ended in pink plastic tennis slippers barely reaching the floor. Her ample lap cradled her right hand, which was thickly swathed in snow-white bandages. Soft-looking bosoms hung over the belt of a pale-blue shirtdress of chambray; there were telltale signs of its having been worn in the kitchen for several days. Her chin rested on her left shoulder while she apparently dozed, so her facial features were hidden from me, even after I realized that it was perfectly safe to stare straight at her.

I was astonished to discover that the old man was, in fact, a frail-looking boy child of some twelve or thirteen years. He was so obviously tense and so marked by whatever it was that life—or human beings—had done to him that both his face and his bony little frame gave the immediate impression of extreme age.

He stared straight ahead, through the doors and down the lengthy hall. His eyelashes, like his close-cropped hair, were almost white, and so thick that his eyes were scarcely visible. Indeed, his left eye seemed to be swollen nearly shut, and blackness rimmed with angry red had settled beneath it. Across his forehead, running from brow to hairline, was a welt about the size of a man's finger; it too was black, with patches of dried blood where the skin had been broken.

I gave up the pretense of reading my newspaper and studied him with a sense of complete impunity. He was obviously unaware of my existence, or that of anyone else in the room except his companion. Yet, I thought I had never seen such alertness; somehow as he sat close beside the woman who would easily make three of him, his back curved forward and his arms resting along the chair arms, he seemed ready in an instant to spring from his chair. The wild force, which I sensed without in any way being able to identify rationally or to apprehend on a personal level, was as palpable as anything I had ever perceived, though I could not validate what I intuited by a single detected movement, even of his eyelids.

A faded jumper jacket was draped over the back of the chair, but his jeans were faded several shades lighter. He couldn't possibly have seen my eyes skim over the jagged slit just above the knee next to the woman—not the kind of fashionable rip one paid extra for, I was sure of that; but he reached for the baseball cap that was lying on the floor near his feet and, without shifting his glance, hung it across that knee. Feeling embarrassed and caught, I bent my gaze once more upon my paper.

Then a coincidence occurred. I had opened the *Herald* to the "Local and Regional News" section and casually scanned an item about a violent incident in the eastern part of the state, the likes of which have become so commonplace that they hardly strike one as newsworthy anymore. An elderly farmer had been transported to Mercy Hospital—this very hospital—after being brutally beaten by three neighbors. One of the three had sworn out a warrant against him on a charge of child molestation. He had allegedly mistreated a niece of these avengers. The name of the victim was. . . .

"Mrs. Harper?"

I jumped. Just as I was reading the name, a doctor had spoken it from only a few feet away. He had come, as he explained, from Intensive Care to report on the progress of the woman's husband—and obviously the boy's grandfather.

They both listened without a word, and neither looked up into the face of the doctor, who stood immediately in front of them.

"Mr. Harper is doing as well as can be expected right now. He's very sore, and we can't do anything about the broken ribs except try to keep him fairly comfortable. We're going to do some checking to see whether there's internal bleeding, and I'll keep you informed." He turned to leave, then added, "Meanwhile, just try to calm him down when you visit."

He smiled with his mouth and touched the boy on the shoulder before walking out of the room with long steps and disappearing down the dim hall. The boy didn't respond to the touch, and for several minutes they both just stared straight ahead and kept their thoughts to themselves.

By now several people had congregated in our section of the room, and several standing or sitting close by had listened unabashedly to the doctor's report. Everybody always stopped chatting and waited breathlessly when a doctor appeared in the doorway or when the telephone at the attendant's desk rang. Relief and a return to conversation followed the sound of someone else's name. We were all too engrossed in our individual concerns to entertain sympathy untempered by a kind of hard comparison to our own woes. There was nothing in this stage of the Harper story that would have caused an undue stir.

After a while the woman seemed to sense that she had our attention, though up to that time she had shown no signs of being aware of our presence. I don't think she could have noticed the passing of a newspaper among those sitting across from us. It must simply have been the time when she had to weave together some words to make a kind of buffer for the ineffable.

She took her left hand and gingerly used it to shift the other one in her lap. Glancing almost timidly at the boy and then looking straight ahead of her, as before, she began. Her voice surprised me by its strength and by its youthfulness. Just listening without seeing her, I would have conjured up a very different picture—perhaps a picture closer to what, under other circumstances, she might have been like.

"I reckon he's lucky to be alive," she said, without her tone modulating up or down. Then she reached over to touch, very tentatively and gently, the mark on the boy's forehead.

"Me'n him, too," she added.

"Were you-all beaten up too?" asked one of the listeners. "That's not mentioned here." She tapped the paper which was loosely folded on her knee.

Mrs. Harper leaned forward a little, and the boy's back stiffened.

"They put it in the paper? Well, what happened is bound to be spread all over, I reckon."

We waited while she contended with some thoughts I couldn't even imagine, though I couldn't help trying. Finally she decided to go on.

"I watched 'em beatin' on Boley as long as I could stand it, and him already flat on the floor and his blood spurtin' everywhere. So I just grabbed old Luster's arm as he was liftin' it again to whale Boley with that backer stick. Well, sir, he just sort of shook me off like I wasn't no more than that little old feist pup of ours or a fly, and he sent me spinnin' 'way across the room. I guess I'm lucky this old noggin's harder than the chifforobe."

She laughed a little and let her fingers inspect the back of her head as if that was the first time she had give this ailment a thought.

"Then while Buster took over hittin' Boley and stompin' on him with his manurey old brogans, Luster stooped down over me till that empty socket of his was right in my face, I thought I would vomink for sure. . . ."

"Empty *eye socket?*" somebody blurted out for all of us. I couldn't have asked. The horror of it made me cringe.

"Lord, yes, he went up to Veterans, wasn't long ago, and they lifted his whole entire eye out. Said it was injured in Vietnam or something. I think he's crazy in his head from over there, is what I think. But that's no excuse. And he won't cover it up, I think out of pure-dee meanness. That's a sight I won't forget. Naw, Buster's his twin, but he ain't crazy that way—he's just plain mean. I guess that's why they wouldn't have him in the army."

"How'd old Luster get in if they don't want mean 'uns?" The boy spoke in a monotone, reminding us that he was there, and listening too.

"Law, I don't know, Roger Dale. Don't ask me to explain the gov'ment, Son. All I know is, they's mean as snakes, the whole batch of 'em, and they aim to do us dirt. That's what he said when he stuck that sinkhole down over my face and breathed right on me. 'Polly Harper, we're gonna get you and your old man too.' And he spit out some more filth that I wouldn't repeat even in a room by myself.

"After that he stood up and planted a brogan square on top of my hand and tromped down on it and then just ground it in. I couldn't hardly see, that pained me so much, but right then Roger Dale snatched hisself from old Earl, Jr., was holdin' him over by the front door, and in a blink he was ridin' old Buster's back like a young wild cat. You wouldn't believe."

She paused and looked proudly at the boy beside her, but he was gazing off down the hall as if he weren't listening.

"Well, Luster just reached over with that backer stick he'd been usin' and gives Roger Dale a lick up side of his head that made him turn loose. Would have anybody. It popped like a firecracker.

"I reckon they figured they'd done their do, so they took their sticks and stomped on outside, all three of 'em, tellin' each other what else they ought to do. I heard their old rattle-trap take off down the road."

I think it was the grotesque image of the eye that removed from the now rapt audience any compunction about showing an open and unabashed interest. I shuffled as far as I could into the corner of my chair and almost managed to take the scene before me as an imaginative intrusion rather than a flesh-and-blood encounter. The polite reticence which we ordinarily affected regarding the misfortune of others somehow didn't seem called for in this case. Mrs. Harper's narrative had moved us into a realm beyond the ordinary and the real. It was the kind of stuff we heard pouring shamelessly from ready mouths of talk show guests—victims and victimizers all lined up to appall and to entertain us millions asking to be horrified by problems that shrank our own to the size of mundane grievances. Thanks to those confessionals offered before glaring cameras, we had learned to tolerate the intolerable, and we could do so without pain because the very grotesqueness created a cushion, a shield, an awful antitype of esthetic distance. By revealing to us the beginnings of a story too violent and inhuman to touch us where our own hearts and pulses lurked in sanctuary, Mrs. Harper had delivered her trauma over into the realm of public domain. As for Roger Dale, he didn't seem to be affected by the telling, one way or the other.

"It seemed like hours till the ambulance and the police got there," Mrs. Harper continued, calmly and matter-of-factly, never addressing any one member of her audience. Now and then, she shifted in her chair a little, as if she were uncomfortable. "Roger Dale, he explained, and I helped all I could, but Boley, he was just layin' on the floor bein' sick all over hisself and the rug and all. My hand was bleedin' like a stuck pig, and Roger Dale took and wrapped an old pillow slip around it before the others got there. Throbbed like a dratted toothache all the time we was bein' slung around in that ambulance. 'Course, me and Roger Dale we rode in the cab, and all the time we was wonderin' would

Boley last all the way to the hospital. Well, he did. Soon as they rolled him off somewhere to work on him, they started to patch us up in the Emergency Room."

About that time the attendant announced that it was time for the nine o'clock visit, and I realized with surprise that several minutes had passed without my worrying about Erna and what I would do about overseeing her recovery while going on with my own life. I gave my head a little shake to restore my focus on reality. I rose hastily and joined the crowd, which moved as one through the door and down the hall, silent with dread or anticipation. Roger Dale supported his grandmother by holding his bony little hand under her left elbow and slowing his steps to accommodate her halting shuffle.

Because I lingered a few moments to discuss arrangements for my sister's imminent transfer from Intensive Care, the Harpers were already settled into their same chairs when I reached the waiting room. Mrs. Harper seemed content to sit nursing her bandaged hand without reading or knitting or doing anything except, no doubt, remembering and worrying. It occurred to me that she probably looked unnatural to her grandson, for I suspected that she hadn't had much opportunity in her life just to sit and relax. I briefly considered shifting to the empty chair between me and Mrs. Harper, possibly offering a few words of sympathy. Resisting the impulse, I rummaged in my tote bag for a pen and crossword puzzle book.

"I thought he seemed more like hisself than last night, didn't you, Roger Dale?"

"Yes'm I guess so. He was cussin' strong as ever." The boy hardly parted his lips to answer in a tone that was not disrespectful, not sarcastic, but saturated with a bitter irony far too heavy for a child his age. "Seems like Saturday and Sunday would've got all of that out of him."

Mrs. Harper made no response to his words or to his tone. She merely picked up the narrative thread where she had dropped it.

"Earl, Jr.—that's Luster and Buster's older brother, the one that took out the warrant—he come up late Friday evening, right after feedin' time, and laid it flat on Boley what it was they was accusin' him of doin' to Sally. Well, I expected him to have a stroke right there on the front porch—he wouldn't allow Earl, Jr., up the steps—and he told him to get off his place and stay off. If I hadn't been listening inside the door, I wouldn't a-knowed beans, for Boley wouldn't tell me one thing.

"All the week end, he just took spells of cussin' and rarin'—"

"And traipsing down to the barn," Roger Dale interspersed.

"Yes, agreed his grandmother, and she took time to ponder some things before continuing. "So by Sunday night, with this and that, he was might' nigh wore out. He was sittin' in his old rocker pulled up close to the fireplace, with his legs stretched out till his toes was nearly on the dogirons. He just had on his long underwear and his overhalls with one gallus hangin' down. I 'magine he was about sung to sleep by the fire poppin' and wavin' like it does. Then all of a sudden, they all three busted in, and all of that happened the way I said. Leavin' us all tore up like you see us here. Me and Roger Dale like we are, and Boley all broke up and his two eyes so swole he couldn't hardly tell us from anybody."

She stopped and glanced around at the half dozen or so of us, leaning toward her at various degrees and angles. I had closed my book and begun to listen with full attention in spite of myself. The risk of becoming personally involved was still in my mind, but these two poor souls had stirred in me an emotional response that I seldom admitted.

Mrs. Harper's tone became defensive, I thought. "Boley always worked hard and seen after his own," she declared. "I don't know what I woulda done without my boy here to keep me company while he had to be out and about. I tell you, Wonder Hollow can be mighty dark when the sun goes down and the owls and whip-poorwills set in to arguing back and forth. Electricity helps, it sure does, but a hundred-watt bulb don't seem no more'n a lightnin' bug sometimes."

Roger Dale's face was unusually white, especially for a country boy, but his knuckles were even whiter as he clutched the arms of his chair. It seemed that his grip tightened as his grandmother talked on.

"Poor little Sally Foriest is not a bad girl. Bless her heart, she just don't know where her pillow'll be from one night to the next. Her mama was the only girl in that pile of roughneck boys, and she took off and left her teeny baby. Hasn't been heard of since, as I know of, not even a post card. The three brothers shuffle poor little Sally around, whichever wife needs her the most, to wash and iron and change dirty didies. I seen her ironing shirts when she had to stand on two Sears Roebuck catalogs. And her not much older'n Roger Dale here."

"She's the same age as me, but she's just in the fifth, because she failed two years for missing so much." Roger Dale provided this information without so much as turning his head or shifting his eyes.

She glanced about at her audience, and for the moment it was as if she were entertaining visitors on her front porch; it was as though she had temporarily escaped the memory of her present woes. In spite of her grimy dress and hot-pink shoes—nobody like her had entered my library or my life—I felt a something like admiration fluttering inside me.

"Roger Dale has always gone to school regular. I seen to that. He can help with the work later, when his schooling is took care of, is what I always said, wasn't it, Son? Only time he missed, his daddy took it into his head to sashay through and drag him off on a trip to Memphis. Nothin' else would do him."

"I was in the second grade, and it was only Friday and Monday," he quickly explained, and I was left wondering whether he was defending his absentee father or his own attendance record.

After the twelve-thirty visit, the usual mid-afternoon lull blanketed the room. Later, noisy visitors freshly cut loose from ordinary activities in their real worlds would rush in for the four o'clock visit. Thinking with some relief that this was possibly the last full day that I would have to spend in this room, I curled up in my leather chair, closed my eyes, and tried to relax for a few minutes. I soon gave up, but continued to keep my head back, my eyelids half closed. Two or three people had moved to the sofa which was directly facing the television set, perched high over our heads for widest visibility—or out of the reach of meddling fingers. The machine was in serious need of adjustment, with images distorted out of all recognition. However, based on my own experience, I doubted that many people had noticed the fluttering and zigzagging, for the screen was mostly used for projecting inward dramas and unexpressed anxieties. Only if there came a few moments of silence did heads raise to see what had gone wrong.

Mrs. Harper spoke in a low voice to Roger Dale, and without a word he arose and helped her to pull herself out of the snug chair and make her way to the restroom door at the far end of the room. His back was toward us as he waited, and through my now wide open eyes I studied his pathetically narrow shoulders and thin body.

As he assisted her back to her chair, she said, quite cheerfully, "They's a place on my hip as big as my hand and black as an old iron skillet." It was almost as if she had been presented a medal to validate the reality of her experience.

For a long while the Harpers and everyone else in the room were nearly out of my consciousness; then a movement attracted my attention. Roger Dale had raised up from his chair just far enough to reach a discarded morning paper left lying on a chair across from him. It was, I could tell, still folded to the section where his family's sordid story was told.

He held the paper close to his face, so I couldn't see his expression as he read; I very much doubted that there was one.

But suddenly he grasped his grandmother's arm. She must have been dozing, for she jumped and grunted.

"Mamaw, it says here they're still 'at large.' The police said— they *promised*—they'd get 'em, for sure, and it says right here, 'AT LARGE.'"

His voice became shrill and loud for the first time, and his finger trembled as he planted it under each word of the article, reading it aloud to Mrs. Harper.

"My land," was all she said, but that was enough. She repeated it, her good hand all the while stroking the bandaged one.

"I'm never going back there," Roger Dale announced with as much strength and finality as any grown man could have mustered.

Now it was Polly Harper who was helpless and terrified, but who had to try to calm her grandson.

"What do you 'magine, that we'll set up housekeeping at the Holiday Inn?" she asked him with a feeble attempt at playfulness.

"I'm sorry about your quilts and your albums and my books and baseball cards, but I'm not going back to Wonder Hollow as long as I live. *And I don't mean for you to go either.*"

He turned his neck and shot her one blazing look before fastening his gaze again on the door and what was beyond it. Knowing that this was no time to attempt an answer, she merely patted his arm and, without looking at anyone, sat very still, obviously enduring the throes of her private misery.

At four o'clock Roger Dale somehow managed to steer his grandmother along fast enough to stay in the midst of the swiftly moving crowd. I soon lost sight and awareness of them, and, since I left for home after a short visit with my greatly improved sister, I was to see them no more that day.

Upon my arrival the next morning at the usual time, my cheerfulness was immediately erased by one glance that revealed the appalling change which had occurred in Roger Dale in so few hours. His face had grown paler by several degrees—something I would not have thought possible—and his cheek bones made shiny slashes as chalk-white as his knuckles. For the first time, I could see, between thick white lashes, slits of eyes like clear water turned to blue ice. If he had seemed alert before, he was many times more so now; it was as if his whole being were concentrated into an effort to penetrate to the very end of the dusky hall, to extend his vision even farther to wherever lurked that enemy allowed to roam "at large," stalking him and his grandmother until that inevitable tragic hour.

Mrs. Harper was sleeping in the chair close beside him, and little puffs of breath blew a loose wisp of gray hair up and down near her cheek. I was certain that Roger Dale had not closed his eyes once, but I could see that he was reaching the limits of self-willed endurance as exhaustion gnawed at his nerves and brain.

There was a quiet underflow of conversation and the crackling of newspapers and above it all the babbling of cheerful voices floating down from the television set. Roger Dale must have dozed in spite of himself, for he leaped wildly from his chair just as a man in denim coveralls pushed open the door. In a flash he had tackled the man about his knees, and the two were tangled and flailing their limbs on the floor. Everyone stood up, well out of range, watching in disbelief, too astonished to attempt intervention.

Somehow Roger Dale managed to get on top of the man; and, making a vise of his bony knees, he held him down and clutched his neck with both hands, pounding his bald head up and down against the floor, crying and talking in words that could not be understood. All around them on the brown carpet were scattered tools from the man's TV repair kit, which had come open when it was flung against the wall.

Two orderlies ran up the hall and entered the waiting room. Without a word they stooped, one on either side, and began to pry the boy's hands loose from the repairman's neck. I heard a quavering voice say, "Don't hurt the boy!" and then again, more insistently, "Please be careful and don't hurt the boy!" At first I did not realize that it was I who was speaking as I hovered over the tangled mass of humanity.

One of the orderlies held Roger Dale while the other helped the stunned man to his feet. He stared wildly about the room, hardly focusing on any of us amazed onlookers, violently shaking his head from side to side as if to restore sense.

Mrs. Harper, forgetful of her bruised hip and wounded hand, rushed over to embrace Roger Dale, talking into his ear as if they were the only two people in the whole world.

"Now, now, little Budgie, let Mamaw hug her little boy. We'll take care of each other. All right. All right, Budgie."

Above our heads a talk show host was seducing panelists into entertaining the world with shocking revelations of personal aberrations and social malaise. The host, the sofa, and the willing participants were intriguingly mashed and melded into rick-rack designs that undulated like proud flags in a contending wind.

Searching for Self

Philip's Room

*A*ctually, Philip didn't mind staying at Mama and Papa's house. They had always lived at this same place for as long as he had been born, and much longer. When people used to ask him where his hometown was, he couldn't really say, but he began to tell them it was Salem. His mother, LaRue, had grown up here—in this dump, she always said. But when he came for a visit from whatever town he was living in with Paul and LaRue, everything was in the right place, and he knew where that was. It was like coming home to his own room.

In fact, Mama called it "Philip's room" and never touched the things he left there or threatened to sweep them out. When he came, he always brought with him a bulky cardboard box, carefully mended at the corners with brown tape. In it he kept a growing array of glossy or fuzzy pictures of movie stars with their autographs in the corners and sometimes "Love" or "Your friend." There were also some play programs which LaRue often tossed on the hall table, and she didn't care if he had them. A thick lined tablet and his diary stayed underneath the pictures, all private and safe. He would always go straight in and get on his knees to tuck the box under his bed, hidden by the *Gone With the Wind* bedspread which Mama had brought him from Atlanta once, when she went to visit her sick sister.

Some of his favorite pictures were always propped on the dresser opposite his bed so that he could look at them at night when he had trouble going to sleep. And when he opened his eyes in the morning and couldn't remember at first where he was, it helped for Bogart or Bette Davis to give him a wink assuring him that they knew, all right.

It seemed strange, though, to be going to school from Mama and Papa's house. In all the years since he had started to school, he and Paul and LaRue had never lived anywhere near Salem School. So his visits to Mama's had been only on holidays and during summers. A few times Mama had come on the bus with her frayed tapestry suitcase and stayed with him in their house while Paul and LaRue were away on trips. That was not the same as being here, in Mama and Papa's home, but it made things better.

It was pleasantly different to be pulling on his clothes and getting ready for school here, with Mama moving about in the nearby kitchen washing up the dishes from the breakfast she had cooked for him. He stood in front of the bathroom sink and studied the reflection of his face, white under a naked, bright bulb. Wetting his comb, he made his red hair lie down, straight back from his forehead, the way he had decided to train it.

He hadn't noticed anybody else at his new school with red hair. Well, there was Evelyn Crews, but hers was more *orange*, and her freckles were so big and brown you didn't much think about her hair. The boys mostly had dirty blond-brown hair that just looked common. He was glad his hair was special, and he didn't have many freckles; he didn't like to be in the sun that much, and, besides, Mama said it was dangerous for people with his coloring.

He wondered whether there were any redheaded Frenchmen. Would they think he was one of *them* as he strolled down the streets of Paris—*Paree, monsir*—in April? Or would they be amazed that this rich and handsome American could speak their language so well?

The mirror gave him back a debonair smile as he turned to go to his room for his books.

"Merci, merci! Ou *est* the *best* from the *West?*" He repeated the little triple rhyme that he had made while he scooped up his things and stuffed them into his new black shoulder satchel.

"Philip Edward, it's almost time for us to leave," Mama called.

He didn't know why she was taking him to school this morning instead of letting him ride the bus, but he was glad. All he knew was that Miss Hannah had tried to reach his parents at their new home last night, and when no one answered, she had rung up Mama. He had been sitting at the kitchen table leafing through his new geography book and absent-mindedly using a spoon to chase the last of the orange Jell-O Mama had made for him, as always, because she thought it was his favorite. Mama stood with the phone to her ear, leaning against the doorjamb and using her free hand to dust off the top edge of the refrigerator. Then her hand stopped moving, and she just listened, nodding and moving her lips as if she were rehearsing what she would say back to Miss Hannah when it finally came her turn to talk.

Except Philip hadn't known it *was* Miss Hannah until Mama hung up the receiver and told him she would drive him to school in the morning because his teacher wanted to have a conference with her. Philip wondered if all the mothers would be there—looking young with curls and pantsuits and little children hanging onto them. But Mama would have to come for him because LaRue was visiting a friend in Montgomery while Paul was preaching for a week somewhere else.

Philip wondered if Miss Hannah would tell Mama and all the others how he had written the best essay on "My Summer Vacation."

She was standing in the kitchen as he came down the tiny hall; and to him she looked like the portrait of a real lady, framed in a square of light. There was nothing *common* about the way she looked, or ordinary. She wore a gray-and-white voile dress, with a crisp white collar and the cameo he used to love to finger when he was small and she let him sit for as long as he wanted to in her soft lap. The tip of his finger remembered with some kind of sadness the feel of the raised figure, white against black, of the dignified lady in the Scarlett O'Hara skirt.

Mama was pulling on the white kid gloves that she always wore when she went on visits or important errands. She already had on her hat, perched a little to the left and over her eye—her best fall hat, a light gray felt with black grosgrain ribbon encircling it just above the brim and ending in a narrow bow above the "club" she made of her white hair at the back of her neck.

"What will the church sisters think now?" Paul asked LaRue, when she came back from the beauty parlor with her long auburn hair gone and her head looking like a small knob atop her slim, long neck.

Philip had been the first to see, when she came home, with delicious town smells caught in her clothes, and he approached her with awe, feeling somehow that now she was a stranger indeed. His breath almost refused to come when, later, he watched her sitting on the stool in front of her vanity dresser, holding the pretty mirror with its long handle and a lovely swan on the back. Philip was not usually welcome in this room—not in LaRue's and Paul's room. This time he was astonished at his own rashness.

Sometimes at night, in a strange new town where he didn't even know anybody to ask to go to the picture show with him, his room would close in around him until he couldn't even create in his head the beautiful worlds to be free in. Then he would creep to their room and mash his body against the hardness of their closed door. Sometimes he dreamed that they would hear him there and call out—Paul, perhaps—"Come in here, Son, and get under these covers to warm; what're you waiting for?"

Or—LaRue, maybe—"Teddy, come to me this instant. Squeeze in here between Daddy and me."

He would flatten himself against the door and with his own mouth shape their lines for them, and then whisper into the chill air, "Mommy! Daddy!"

Those were words which LaRue never allowed him to use. "You think I want people to decide I'm an old hag ready to crawl off into a corner and fade away? How do you think I'd feel with a long-legged boy like you tagging along and calling me 'Mommy'?" It didn't sound pretty, the way she said it. And she would toss her hair in the air—before she left it all in the beauty parlor to be swept up and thrown into the trash—and raise her pointed chin high as if to dare anyone to disagree. Not for anything would Philip have her know how his whole chest hurt.

As he watched her studying the reflection of her new look in the two mirrors, dipping her chin onto her bosoms and turning first this way and then that, making the little stool squeak beneath, Philip was mesmerized. So great was his awe, his yearning to be admitted into LaRue's consciousness, to be just a pale reflection, alongside her brilliant one, in the shadowy rooms of her mind, that he was drawn, in spite of himself, all the way into her bedroom. His crepe-soled shoes tugged at the wool carpet with its pale blue flowers still as pretty as ever, the bad part that she complained to Paul about completely out of sight under the bed.

He approached where she sat, almost unable to breathe, yet keenly aware of the delicious smell of tea roses that was always wherever she was, and even in the clothes she left on the bathroom floor. She continued to look at herself in the hand mirror, and Philip didn't blame her, so beautiful she was, more beautiful than any movie star. She didn't act as if she could see him. She wet the tip of her finger between her lips and used it to smooth out two little twigs cut short to hang in front of her ears.

As if moving of its own volition, Philip's hand reached slowly upward to the back of his mother's neck, which struck him as a revelation, a forbidden sight such as had never before been revealed to him. He felt his face and ears covering with a flush of shame and something like guilt.

A frightening sensation overwhelmed him as he let his fingers run up the surface of the clipped hair, against its brittle grain. Short whiskers pricked his skin, and a shiver ran through his whole body. The sight and the touch of the two slim bones and the deep valley between them were a mystery and wonder that he could not stand.

LaRue flinched and jerked away from his contact. "Would you stop that, bad boy? What are you doing in my room, anyway?"

Then she pulled the soft flowered robe closer about her shoulders and bent toward the vanity mirror to examine the shape of her eyebrows. Philip tiptoed from the room.

Philip thought the haircut would be another of the things his father wouldn't approve. He was thinking that when Paul came through the front door and dropped onto the floor his big black suitcase, all rounded out with clothes and books. When he went away for a week or two to "hold meetings" for some church, he always took this big bag and carried his thick pulpit Bible under one arm. He looked the same when he went and when he returned. Philip would always picture him this way as he eagerly watched for his return. He would station himself on the front porch, if their house had one; if not, he would loiter in the yard watching for the familiar car to round the corner. He practiced over what he would tell his father in such interesting fashion that he would laugh and laugh. And then Paul would share with him anecdotes about places and people. But he was always tired, and LaRue would call him from their room. Waiting for him to come turned out to be the best part.

On the night after the haircut and Paul's return, Philip had tried especially hard not to hear. He was always relieved when his room was located far away from that of his parents, but it could never be far enough. When they were having loud discussions, he would take out his box of pictures and think about movies; and he would put a big pillow against his headboard and try to bury his ears in the softness. But words always managed to cut through, confusing him and making bad dreams.

Paul's "preacher" voice, not loud but trained to carry, would penetrate the walls and Philip's awareness. Soon LaRue's voice would become louder and mix itself with tears. In spite of all, Philip would catch phrases that were all too clear and familiar. "What will the church sisters think?" ". . . the elders' disapproval . . ." ". . . your unsuitable conduct. . . ." His heart would sink as he listened, for he early learned to expect that soon there would be talk of "relocating," and the packing would start again.

He had learned to let his precious dog collection stay packed, each little glass figure wrapped ever so carefully with wadded sheets of newspaper. Only his favorite few sat on the top of his washstand. The others he unwrapped and wrapped when he felt like visiting them, stroking their china bodies and looking into the uniqueness of each face. Sometimes he would think of Jody and his poor shot deer, and Jane Wyman with her thin mouth that refused to smile.

The most recent move had been the first to bring them near Mama and Papa. Philip was glad, for he could walk to see them; but he was especially happy that he would be nearer town than they, and he could go by himself to the movie theater every Saturday afternoon.

Mama carried a shiny sack from McClure's and set it on the back floorboard as they got into her maroon Chevrolet. Philip thought the car looked all right, but he was ashamed of the seat covers that Mama had made from feedbags, and the seams were stretched so that the black seats showed through. Philip put his book bag at his feet and leaned against the door, feeling the pleasant bite of cold metal against his arm. He hoped they didn't look common.

("Mahster Philip, I will be back for you in the white Rolls this afternoon. Perhaps it would be best if you didn't allow your young classmates to accompany you home this time. They will be disappointed, to be sure, but you must explain to them that your parents have planned a gala evening just for the three of you. They'll understand. No, no, Mahster Philip, I'll escort you to your classroom and carry your bag.")

Riding the battered yellow school bus was an embarrassment to Philip. He always tried to slide into the front seat, behind the driver, and he made an effort to block out the sounds and the smells and the unpleasant brushes of his skin against strange skin. The trips home in the afternoon were the worst. Loud boys jostled each other on purpose, and girls squealed shrilly and pretended to be mad at the boys they liked. By the time he stood up and prepared to swing off the bus, he was nauseated and choked by the odors of sweat emanating from the big boys and dried urine from the clothes of little children who huddled together in the aisle, afraid they would miss their time to get off.

"When I finish at your school, I'm going to take Papa's shirt back to McClure's to exchange. Then I'll go by Gafford's Drugs for Papa's blood pressure medicine and on home."

The street, the street, the street. LaRue, LaRue. "Ou est . . . LaRue?"

That night, at the place before the place they lived now, Philip had tried harder than ever not to hear the voices. He had even taken two pillows and crawled into the back of his closet, crouching on top of his Monopoly set, feeling dangling pants legs tickle his nose in the dark. But no matter how hard he mashed the pillows against his ears, the words still burst through.

"How far do you think you can go? You're no better than a street walker." Did he mean her name? "Don't you think I know what you're up to? Don't you realize everybody'll soon be talking again?"

LaRue was shouting. "Hypocrite! Hypocrite! How long do you think *you* can fool everybody with your fine precious words? And I keep telling you I didn't even *see* Ches Bowman! I'm just so sick and tired!"

Then the talk was back and forth, but lower. Philip wiped his nose on the corner of a pillowcase and pushed his knees into his stomach because he hurt there again, *so much*. Several times he caught the words "the boy," "the boy."

Philip thought Mama looked nice as she walked a little ahead of him up the sidewalk to the front of the school building. With her gloved hands she gave a little tug to each side of her shimmery gray dress. The heels of her black Sunday slippers clicked and made him think of tap dancers. His tennis shoes hardly made a sound.

Only a few children were there already, opening creaking locker doors or lounging sleepily around the water fountain. He didn't think any of them recognized him. Buses hadn't arrived yet to spill out their shoving, shouting hordes.

Mama had already met Miss Hannah. She was the one who had to bring Philip's report card and records from his last school to enroll him in Shiloh Elementary. Miss Hannah spoke to him and suggested that he sit at the reading table near the back of the room while she talked with his grandmother. Miss Hannah pulled one of the small desk chairs closer to her desk for Mama, and they began to talk quietly. To Philip's ears it was mostly a friendly-sounding hum.

The metal of the folding chair was cold under Philip's knees. He rubbed the smooth wood of the little round table and absent-mindedly fingered through the pages of a magazine.

"Mother, may I please have another of those tiny cakes like we had here last Christmas? They were *so* elegant and delicious!"

"Of course, we'll all have some—two each this year, just to celebrate. Who cares if they cost five dollars apiece? Nothing is too good for us!"

"And what are we celebrating, my Love?" Father asked, in the joking tone that made Philip feel good all over.

"Just being together, here in this wonderful place! My two boys and me. Feel that air, and listen to those magic sounds! Was there ever such a place as New York at Christmas? It's magic. *We're* magic!"

"Drat, we're being interrupted," said Father. "Why, hello, Miss Garland. We all loved the musical. We never miss one of *your* opening nights. You remember my wife and my only son?"

"Thank you for asking," said Mother, "but we're just about to stroll around Times Square and sing and be happy. Oh, yes, it *is* a frosty evening, but our furs will keep us warm—and our love, of course!" She laughed and playfully tickled the back of Philip's neck, inside the cozy stand-up fur collar.

"Philip, dear, would you come up here now and join your grand-mother and me?"

Miss Hannah motioned toward a desk near Mama. He saw Mary Lou's pink-and-black plaid notebook inside it as he sat down.

"Miss Hannah tells me that you've been putting 'Paul Thomas Liddell, Jr.,' on your papers, Philip. Why is that, Son?"

Philip raised his shoulders slightly. His sandy lashes dipped to shade his eyes. He didn't answer.

Miss Hannah leaned toward him across her desk. Her eyes skimmed above a stack of spelling workbooks. She moved the cheap vase with artificial flowers that Philip hated and tried not to notice. Then her eyes landed straight on Philip's and wouldn't budge.

"Philip, dear, Mary Lou and Evelyn have told me that you are saying that your real name is Paul and that Philip is the name of your dead brother. Now, we know that this is not true. Don't we, Philip?"

Philip felt Mama sitting stiff-backed in the chair near him. Out of the corner of his eye he saw the two gray mounds made by her knees, which were raised a little because the chair was too low for her. He offered his answer to her rather than to Miss Hannah.

"Yes, Ma'am."

"And you do know that it's wrong to *lie*, don't you, Philip?" Miss Hannah's tone was serious, and she was looking at him as if she didn't even know who he was.

He felt a hot wave of righteous indignation. Forgetting to whom he was speaking, he used a harsh tone that sounded strange, and yet strangely familiar, to his ears.

"Of course I know. My father's a minister. I can show you where it is in the Bible." He made as if to stand, glaring at her in his fury.

Mama reached out a gloved hand to touch him on his knee. She spoke to Miss Hannah as if he were not present.

"I'll be sure to talk with Philip. He's a very intelligent boy, and he'll understand. I think you'll find him to be a more than satisfactory pupil."

Miss Hannah stood up. Now she was talking cheerfully, as if she were glad for the conference to be over and everything settled.

"Oh, I already know that. Philip has an excellent mind and a fine imagination. He's going to be one of my best English scholars. And he has been so fortunate to be able to travel so extensively with his parents. Did you accompany them to New York last summer, Mrs. Grainger?"

Mama picked up her purse from the floor and lifted herself out of the little chair. For one second her eyes met Miss Hannah's and barely flickered. But she merely said, "No, I'm afraid I've never seen New York."

"Well, neither have I, but Philip's fine essay made me feel as though I *had* been there."

She thanked Mama for coming and walked as far as the door with her. By now Philip's classmates were coming in, talking loudly as they fell into their seats and began to unpack their bags. Mary Lou stared indignantly at Philip, and he quickly arose and moved to his own desk across the aisle.

Miss Hannah didn't pay any special attention to him for the rest of the day. He knew the answers to all of the questions she directed to him. He fancied that Evelyn looked across the aisle at him, with the little red flecks showing in her eyes and matching her hair; she was hoping he would stumble on some answer and reveal his ignorance. But he was more than prepared, for he had already gone through most of his new books. He especially enjoyed poring over the geography book. Already he had skimmed through to see which chapters he could anticipate with the greatest pleasure. He didn't look forward to the chapter on Africa, though Katharine Hepburn *had* made it a bit more inviting. England was all right. But Paris and New York were *the* places: they had *magic!*"

He had watched *An American in Paris* three times, twice on the same Saturday. Gene Kelly helped him escape into such a carefree world that he could almost forget the dingy, small-town movie house with its common smell of old wood and stale popcorn. For those few hours he almost believed he never would have to go outside and blink to get used to the light as he trudged down dreary streets to the sad-looking, still-strange house where Paul and LaRue would be, but not especially waiting for him.

"I've got rhythm," he sang in his heart with Gene.

"Philip, may I ask what is the purpose of that scuffling noise you are making with your feet? You are causing a disturbance."

Miss Hannah didn't wait for an answer, but turned her back to the class and continued to fill the board with fractions and whole numbers.

Philip had decided to memorize a poem about a dog which he had discovered in his language book. He liked to memorize songs and poems so that he could say them over to himself in the dark if he couldn't sleep. He knew all the words to dozens of songs from musicals he had seen. Sometimes he sang them aloud to himself when he was going over the autographed pictures he had collected.

Eight lines about a dog presented no challenge at all. He thought about all the china dogs in his collection, and it occurred to him that he would dedicate this poem to his favorite, one which had been to given to him—as had most—by Mama. This one, the largest of all, was always unpacked when they moved to a new place and set where they could look at each other. Mama had told him this dog had been the very favorite of her own son, LaRue's brother that she had never mentioned to Philip in his whole life. He had died of some disease called *croup* and was buried under a big pine tree in the Grainger cemetery. He and Mama and Papa took flowers up there sometimes when Mama said she wanted to.

Philip didn't know what Uncle Morris had called the dog, but he had named him Flicka. Philip was certain that Paul would never agree for him to have a horse. Anyway, it would be too cruel to drag him from stable to stable and force him to get used to new places all the time.

Mary Lou looked a little like Jeanette MacDonald, Philip thought. Out of the corner of his eye he watched her bending over her pretty notebook, writing spelling sentences for tomorrow. Her little pointed chin was close to the paper, and she put out her lower lip to blow a blond cloud of hair from in front of her eyes. He started to wonder whether she might go with him on Saturday to see an old Garbo movie, *Grand Hotel*. Well, he'd probably rather see it by himself again, anyway. If he asked, she would just repeat the hateful rhyme she had chanted at him before, while all the others laughed:

Red-headed peckerwood
Sitting on a fence,
Trying to make a dollar
Out of fifteen cents!

"I have never been so tired in my life," he repeated Garbo's words in his head, suddenly weighed down by the weariness of an old man. He reached under the desk to rub both legs, above his knees; they were starting to ache again.

Last week, when he came out of the theater after seeing *Clash by Night,* a lady from their new church was walking by with a bumpy red net grocery bag in each hand. She stopped in the middle of the sidewalk when she noticed who he was. She stared up at the posters advertising the picture, and her lips moved as she read the name. She glared at the nice color posters of Barbara Stanwyk and Paul Douglas, then—with her nose flared wide—back at Philip.

"Young man, you have *no* business looking at that filth! You're Brother Liddell's little boy, aren't you? Do your parents know where you are right this minute?"

He thought it best to answer, "No, Ma'am." She put her feet down hard with each step on the concrete. As she stomped on down the street, she kept muttering and shaking her head.

He wondered if she would say something to Paul on Sunday, when she stopped at the door to shake his hand, peering at him from behind the thick veil which had captured Philip's interest from the very first Sunday they were here.

He wondered if she had seen *Clash by Night.* Why was she so upset, anyway? He certainly knew all about adultery. It was in the Bible, wasn't it?

While he was crouched on the front seat of the school bus, ready to jump off when it was time, and later, as he walked up the lane between fields of cows munching hay, Philip worried only a little about whether Mama would bring up the visit with

Miss Hannah. He was fairly sure that she wouldn't: she hardly ever bothered him about things. Sometimes he wondered why.

Once when Mama and Papa were sitting at the breakfast table and he wasn't ready to get up yet, he had heard them talking. Mama had said, "I just feel sorry for the poor little orphan." He had lain for a while in his soft, warm nest, pondering her meaning. He decided that she might have been talking about someone else. Yet sometimes he caught her giving him a soft, sad look that almost seemed damp.

Mama hardly ever spoke harshly to anyone. At her house Philip could go to bed without worrying about hateful sounds penetrating the walls of his room and, later, coming back all mixed into bad dreams.

It was only on days when Papa went to Clarksdale for cattle sales and came home late that Mama would act like someone else and make Philip uneasy. He would watch her grow quiet and stiff-faced as the dark closed in; he could tell that she was listening hard for the rattle of Papa's truck and then the slam of the door. When he did come, she would suddenly act too busy to look up from her work at the sink or talk to him. Philip noticed that, on these occasions, Papa would bring with him into the kitchen a strange, *sour* smell, and he thought that might have something to do with Mama's displeased look and sharp tone. Finally, she would set each bowl of food from the warming shelf onto the table with a thump and, saying she wasn't hungry anymore, leave him to eat alone while she went to the back of the house to turn down their bed. She always let Philip go ahead and eat at the regular time, so he would just sit in a chair across from Papa and watch him chew as if he didn't really know what his mouth was doing. In a little while he would scrape back his chair and go out the backdoor and down to the barn. He would still be outside when Philip went to bed.

Once when he was still awake and working on the movie that he was writing, he did hear Mama and Papa—well, actually

Mama—talking in their bedroom after Papa had come back from the barn. He pictured Mama in her nightgown with ruffles at the neck and sleeves, putting away Papa's town pants and folding things to make the room neat for the night. And Papa was probably sitting on the side of the bed in his night shirt, studying his feet. Philip thought he heard one shoe clump to the floor and then in a minute the other one. He knew Mama would stoop to pick them both up and place them side by side on the floor of the closet. From memory he added to the scene the aroma that he loved—the nice old fragrance that wafted out into the room when she opened and closed the closet door.

Mama's voice was low, and rougher than her real voice was—as though something had stuck in her throat. Philip held his pencil still over his script so that he could hear. She kept saying something about "the boy," "that poor boy," ". . . in front of that poor child," and—he thought she said—"that blessed little orphan." That caused him to wonder again what she could mean. He had Paul and LaRue, so she couldn't be calling *him* an orphan, could she?

Then the house grew really quiet, except for a creak somewhere in the old walls, and Philip knew that they were both stretched on the big brass bed, making two long mountains under the old quilt that had real people's names embroidered in different-colored squares.

Once, when rain was coming down against his window and making a roar on the old tin roof, Philip flung back his covers and tiptoed past the bathroom to listen at the door of the other bedroom. At first he could hear not a sound, and the old terror that was always ready to reach out and grab him started to clutch at his throat and make his heart thunder in his ear. Then he heard the long regular sounds of two people breathing in the dark, and shaking with relief he crawled back into bed and soon found sleep.

At times when he couldn't sleep, he would drag the box from under his bed and work on the movie. However, he didn't often have trouble going to sleep at Mama's. The movie work was mostly at Paul and LaRue's.

He had begun it almost a year ago. It was while they lived at McLean, before they knew they would be moving again. Already, almost half of his big tablet was filled with small writing, and he wasn't nearly to the end yet.

He hadn't figured out exactly what was going to happen, but he knew he could make the characters do and say whatever he chose, and he felt happy to exercise his power to see that everything turned out right.

As he plotted and composed speeches, he considered whom he should ask to play the roles; he concluded that it would be wise to wait until after he had finished. Katharine Hepburn was always in his mind as a great possibility, but she might be a bit old for the starring role. He was seriously thinking of Paul Douglas for the father's part, and he kept an image of him in his head as he envisioned each scene.

Many scenes were set in a lavish home, with the mother, the father, and their only son. He wrote small parts for a number of other children; he might use some of his classmates or some of the children from Sunday school, if he decided he liked any of them. He presumed from the beginning that he would take the role of the son. He purposely described him as red-haired and smart.

He loved writing the scenes where the mother and father sat in matching chairs drawn up to a glowing fireplace, while the son sprawled on the floor leaning his head against the father's knee. They would stop in the midst of a discussion and ask him to voice an opinion, and then they would both lean toward him and listen attentively. They would nod and smile at each other as if they were proud, and the father would reach down to ruffle his son's hair.

Soon, at the mother's suggestion, the boy would invite his friends to come over and share the special cookies that she herself had made, without the assistance of the cook. And she talked to them and insisted that it was all right to sit on the good furniture and touch any of her beautiful things. (For scenes like this, he wrote in directions for including floods of soft light and happy, dancy music throughout.)

Lately he had turned to the pages almost to the back of his tablet and begun to work on the final scenes. When the ending was clear, he had decided, then he would know the necessary parts for leading up to it. He had finished most of it in his head and written detailed notes. He would feel better when this part was finished; he wouldn't feel so tired then, and he could proceed to write the wonderful, long sections set in New York and Paris.

He had gotten the idea for the ending while visiting Mama's son's grave, up there on its own little hill under the black-green pine tree. Since they had moved near Mama, he found himself thinking about Uncle Morris a lot, even in the daytime, and he kept wondering if Mama did too. He wondered if her heart hurt sometimes, and when she would get quiet, he would peer closely at her to see if he could discern signs of her suffering.

Even when he was at home, at the new house with Paul and LaRue, he would find himself envisioning that spot. Under the low limbs there was soft, quiet darkness, even when the sun glared on fields adjoining the graveyard and reflected off the backs of grazing cows. When rain fell and penetrated the thick needle canopy, surely it would make only a gentle spray to freshen the moss that grew over the low mound.

In his tablet the last scene was still sketchy, but in his head it became increasingly clear as he went over and over it. It was more real to him that the people and voices and commands that threaded in and out of his consciousness as he brushed against real life. The mother and father would be standing close together, with arms wrapped tightly about each other. They would look down upon the grave that didn't seem at all like a grave because of the piles of lavish, elegant yellow roses concealing any raw dirt. Standing at the head of the grave, caressed just slightly by the lowest pine branches, was a glorious marble statue of their son, all white and shining, his arms outstretched as if to embrace his parents. (At the end, a brilliant spotlight would focus on the statue and then spread out to engulf all three, the son and the parents, with their heads touching, oblivious to the slanting rain. Violin music and then the sounds of a whole orchestra would fill the largest theater with such harmony that no one would ever, ever forget!)

By the day of Mama's visit to the school, Philip had decided that he was ready to tackle the New York scenes and work his way toward the conclusion. That evening, after supper and after Mama hadn't said anything, he first sprawled on his bed to complete his homework; most of the assignments he had done during recess period at school, when the others were romping on the playground, screeching out each other's name close under the windows of Miss Hannah's room. It was hard to concentrate.

Stacking his books on the floor, he turned off the ceiling light and sat with only the round circle of yellow from a bedside lamp glowing on his script tablet. After pausing for a few minutes, he wrote the directions for the beginning of the Waldorf scene. He was pretty sure that he would use Jeanette MacDonald and Nelson Eddy for this scene. So much singing and dancing—and hugging! But before he had finished an entire page, he closed the tablet, for he was so weary that it wasn't going well at all.

Before attempting sleep he had to write in his diary. He had never missed a single day since Mama gave it to him for his birthday. She had mailed it to him at Selah, where they had lived before moving to McLean, with a note saying she hoped it would "be company" for him. When they moved from McLean to this place, he had held his box in his lap, not trusting his pictures or his diary to the movers.

Philip thumbed through the little brown book that was by now scuffed like a comfortable old shoe—and even smelled a little like one. On the first page he had printed in large capital letters: "PHILIP EDWARD LIDDELL'S BOOK. DON'T DARE TURN THIS PAGE!"

The first entry was dated the very next day after the birthday on which he had received the book: October 11, 1951.

"I wonder how many days that makes?" he said to himself. He started to count the pages, but decided to figure instead.

Then he began his entry. "This is about 700 times. I can write better than I could, and spell better too. Miss Hannah says I am her best writer."

He sat for a few minutes, thinking and rubbing the top of his pen absently against his cheek, forming invisible circles and loops. Many times he did not recount a single incident in an entry, but instead recorded questions and thoughts to ponder more later.

He next wrote, "Mama came to my school. I was so embarrassed!" ('Two r's and two s's," he whispered.)

He laid his pen down as if he were finished. He didn't always use all of the page, much less the back. Saturday was always the longest, for he told about the movie and who was in it and how he felt. Often, the last sentence had to bend and run up the side of the full sheet.

Sunday entries were likely to be much more arid. He usually recorded the title of Paul's sermon—like, last Sunday. "The Goodness and Severity of God." He went on to write, "Sunday school was BORING!! Mary Lou smelled like BABY POWDER. LaRue's big hat from Montgomery is elegant, I hope Paul thinks so too, even if it did cost a fortune. I sat between Mama and LaRue. Papa doesn't like church much. He sinks way down in the pew and studies his Sunday slippers that you can nearly see yourself in."

Here he drew a thick black line across the page to separate what he had written from what was to follow.

He bore down so hard that a small puddle of ink came out and spread into a blot. He wrote, "Is a hypocrite the *worst?*"

He chewed on the top of his pen a long time before starting to write again.

"I think it's going to rain again. My head hurts awful bad, and both of my legs do too. *I don't know what's wrong with me.*"

"Was Miss Sadie Thompson a real person?"

"Am I an orphan?"

"Is he a ruey?"

"PS. I don't know who I like."

"PPS. I think Mama likes me. Would she cry?"

He closed the book and carefully placed it in the box underneath pictures that glowed and smiled toothily up at him. Then he clicked off the lamp and, pulling his knees up to his chest, tried to go to sleep fast.

The Quantity of Mercy

*B*efore the air brakes on the dusty Greyhound had ceased to squeak and huff, Brother Billy Rucker had already leaped out to land on the brick sidewalk and look around at a scene that was pleasantly familiar. Nothing much had changed in Shiloh since the first time he stepped from a bus onto its Main Street, uneasy at the prospect of conducting his very first gospel meeting.

That was exactly five years ago. He had been a sophomore in college, years away from Seminary, but eager to begin the work to which he felt called. Every year the people assured him that he didn't look a day older; with his white-blond hair, blue eyes, and fair skin, he would probably look much the same for decades. But on this day, he felt a confidence and assurance which had taken time and experience to attain. He was convinced that these brethren accepted him without reservations, and he looked forward to meeting their needs while at the same time renewing fond acquaintances. For him, this one week of the year was a kind of spiritual retreat into rare Edenic simplicity, away from the controversy and endless sophisticated arguments about good and evil in which his colleagues engaged with alacrity. He, on the other hand, was made nervous by conversations which delved into theological intricacies and, indeed, a religion by which he felt downright threatened.

Dangling a suit bag over one shoulder and clutching a well-scuffed and lumpy satchel in the other, he glanced around to get his bearings and to savor what felt like a homecoming. His quick scan didn't reveal any change except that a variety store had sprung up down the street from Mr. Gafford's drugstore, with only the narrow telephone office separating them. The name of Hardin's Creamery and Hatchery could still be seen, like a ghost, behind the newly painted letters. He guessed the birds would thin out now that the hatchery wasn't there with its discarded seed sacks in the alley.

At the same moment two people called out "Brother Billy," and he set down his satchel to wave to Mr. Walter Gafford. At the same time, Betty Curtis, the telephone operator, leaned out of the open door of her narrow office and called out a welcome to the preacher. Though they had worked here in town for as long as he had been coming to Shiloh—and much longer, he knew—they were in his mind clear and perfect representatives of the membership of the Disciples Band—simple, honest rural folk whose hearts were soft toward messages of love and uprightness, and who were easily touched by the gentlest reminders of possible weaknesses; for their weaknesses were actually no more than mere human frailties which to them loomed large in so blessed a setting.

Mr. Gafford tossed his luggage into the trunk of a shiny blue Plymouth, which was just in front of his store, and Betty waved a quick goodbye as they climbed in. As they drove off, he waved again as he saw her peering through her plate glass window while reaching for wires.

Brother Billy eagerly inquired about some of the ones he remembered most fondly, and Mr. Gafford began to fill him in as they left town and sped down the wide gravel road that led to his house, only a few miles from the town. Soon they passed the New Shiloh Baptist Church, with its narrow tower and bell; just a few hundred yards farther and on the other side of the road was the modest weatherboard structure in which the Disciples Band met. Beaming out at passers-by from two tree trunks was Brother Billy himself on large posters with the date of the revival and the word "WELCOME" in huge letters.

As Brother Billy well knew, the community was firmly and sometimes warmly divided between the Baptists and the Disciples Band. (The Methodists, secure in their old brick structure in the edge of the residential section of Shiloh, generally left these two groups to their own devices.) Even those who had no plans to join up with either group felt called upon from time to time to "take sides." So, in spite of placards and diligent efforts on the parts of faithful members to advertise, not much crossing of the road was anticipated, even though Brother Billy had become familiar to most local citizens and received friendly greetings on the street from outsiders, who needed no help from the biased sisters to decide that he was well-meaning and devoid of guile.

"Brother Billy never had a bad thought in his life," the members would say, never dreaming of raising a contradiction, but just taking pleasure in saying it.

"And he can stand up there in the pulpit looking just like one of the Lord's chosen angels and preach the *sweetest* sermons you would ever want to hear."

The Baptists and most others who weren't counted as "regulars" took Brother Billy's preaching expertise for granted. As for the Baptists, they had their spiritual appetites filled to their satisfaction. In the past there had been some difficulty when the rival congregations scheduled annual revivals for exactly the same week. Though neither group expected support from the other, each felt that its efforts had somehow been hampered by this conflict in time. Furthermore, when the wind was right, Brother Billy's sermon was likely to be interspersed by Miss Grace Luke's locally famous country alto being wafted down the road and through opened windows. So a friendly arrangement was made whereby the Baptists would hold their meeting the second week in July and the Disciples the third. July was considered by all to be the ideal month, for two reasons: farm work was in a comparatively slack stage, leaving the rural members sufficiently rested to attend services for eight straight evenings, and, according to a folk maxim, "It don't rain nights in July"—an assertion sometimes belied by such strenuous pounding on the tin roof as to drown out whole sections of the preacher's sermon, turning him into what looked like a pantomimist striving to entertain a rather distracted audience.

Mrs. Gafford—Miss Lizzie—was watching for the car, and she met the two men on the front steps, hugging Brother Billy and beginning to talk breathlessly while her husband took the bags down the hall. Brother Billy was sincerely glad to see the Gaffords again. He felt that he knew them best of any of the members since they were always elected to house him, the reason being that they had an extra bathroom and a nice quiet bedroom where he could enjoy privacy for studying during the day as well as a comfortable place to sleep.

Revival time was truly Miss Lizzie's period of ascendancy, for she was clearly the unquestioned authority on all matters pertaining to the visiting preacher. Chatting and fanning each evening while the crowd gathered, she could and did show the greatest familiarity with Brother Billy's habits and tastes, from the degree of hardness which he preferred in his breakfast eggs to the interesting fact that he *always* took two baths a day—night and morning. During the week before the preacher's arrival and the opening of the revival, she willingly offered suggestions regarding dishes to be brought to the dinner-on-the ground on Sunday, reminding the other ladies of Brother Billy's special preferences. She, of course, would bring her fresh apple cake, since Brother Billy wouldn't think he was in Shiloh if she didn't.

By bedtime that Saturday of Brother Billy's arrival, the Gaffords had thoroughly filled him in regarding the events that had transpired since last year's revival. Two of the members had passed on, one or two families had moved away from the Shiloh community, but mostly, they were thankful to report, everything was exactly the same. They did hint, in lowered confidential tones, that a few of the members had grown somewhat lax in attendance, and one or two—reluctantly identified by name— had stooped to bringing reproach upon the congregation by committing *public* disgraceful acts.

"This is certainly not gossip, Brother Billy. You know Walter and I better than that. But you do need to be prepared so you'll say the right thing to touch their hearts."

Miss Lizzie, thus concluding this initial orientation period, arose and set about pouring Brother Billy a tall glass of cold milk, having concluded from something he said during his first visit to Shiloh that he enjoyed such a drink just before retiring.

"I understand," he assured her, inwardly praying that he would be given the wisdom to choose the right words to entice wandering brothers and sisters back to the fold and to the safe centrality of the faith. At the same time, he couldn't help being thankful, as he often was, that his calling had been to Shiloh and other places like it. He would be at a loss, he was certain, in a large city church where the human heart fed on sin in its grossness, dramatized its vile nature by deeds that his head could contemplate only in vague terms, while his heart repudiated them. He empathized with these folk, whose childlike hearts suffered twinges for wrongs that were exaggerated because of their tenderness of conscience. Their sins, if sins, were largely those of omission merely, and he needed only to share with them the encouraging, bolstering Word.

As the hour for services drew near on Sunday morning, the little building rocked with the noise and excitement of a family reunion. Children and grandchildren had come home to Shiloh for the grand occasion, and greetings were unrestrained. Tiny little forms loose from otherwise occupied guardians plunged up and down the center aisle shouting to "Mawmaw" and "Pawpaw," who were equally loud in their fond responses.

Brother Billy stood near the door to greet each one who entered, having his hand mashed between the strong calloused paws of farmers and being hugged by flowery-smelling ladies who giggled self-consciously that they reckoned they were old enough to get away with it. Brother Billy's fair skin blushed right up to the edge of his almost white hair, and the delighted sisters moved on up the aisle to repeat what they had said to him and to describe his response.

It was a matter of fond discussion that Brother Billy was unworldly—above and beyond the facts of life, they said, but dotingly, as if he were a child to be protected from what they lived with every day.

Several older members managed to find a moment to mumble in his ear the identity of one who needed for some reason to be given special attention, and Brother Billy, with the sincerity which drew them to him, vowed to do what he could.

Every lady who came in soon noticed the surprising presence of Miss Hattie Fleet, a long-time member of the Baptist Church, and there was a voluble undercurrent of excitement as the news spread on wings up and down both sides of the aisle. Heads turned and fingers fluttered little welcomes. Two of the ladies rose from their seats near the front to go back and embrace her. Miss Lizzie Gafford, one of these, continued to the back to whisper to Brother Billy about how Miss Hattie was mad as a wet hen at Miss Grace Luke over something she had said about her singing, and she just might never set foot in the Baptist Church again. So her soul was full ripe for winning to their persuasion if he only handled it right, Miss Lizzie declared, tapping his shoulder with her fan for emphasis.

Brother Billy's heart fluttered as he rose to speak, and his mouth felt so dry that he had to pour a glass of water from the cool fogged pitcher placed in readiness on the side of the lectern. The burden of responsibility weighed heavily upon him, as it always did when he faced a group of dear people wanting his help and encouragement. He felt drained by the force of their reaching hungrily to pull from him sustenance and direction.

He began to speak fervently, reading from the Bible, then continuing to hold it open before him. He was persuasive in his insistence that the key to goodness and salvation was simple acceptance of the Word, that anyone who *willed* himself—or herself—to be pure and loving found ease in carrying out God-approved resolutions. Perspiration glistened on his forehead, but he was spurred on by nods of approval and understanding. He laid his Bible on the lectern to remove his coat, and Brother Foster, the visiting song director, leaped up to take it and place it, neatly folded, on the front seat beside his own.

Finally finished, Brother Billy, his voice now husky, pled for sinners to come forward during the singing of the invitation hymn. On the first phrase, two of the Miller boys—still looked upon as boys though in their thirties—started down the aisle, bumping into each other like gawky calves in the barnyard, and Brother Billy hurried to meet them in the aisle and escort them to the front seat, where they sat close together beside the folded coats.

Brother Billy knew Lem and Wes, for one or both of them had made public confession of sins every year that he had preached at Shiloh. He felt that they suffered under the weight of a delicate and over-sensitive conscience, and he yearned to instill in them an overpowering awareness of grace, whose power was a blanket to cover every paltry departure from the narrow path.

The moment church services were over, a crowd surged forward to hug and pat the Miller boys, their hope for them having welled up in annual revival. Sister Miller, the boys' mother, was on the verge of fainting, as she was wont to do upon emotion-filled occasions, and Wes had to support her while somebody fanned her till the black butterflies on her veil seemed sure to take flight.

Brother Billy remembered that Wes had been among the missing last year, and he observed that his face now looked strained and older, with dark bags protruding beneath blood-streaked eyes that were intent upon avoiding contact with anyone's glance, especially Brother Billy's. But he reached out to place a sympathetic hand on his bony shoulder. Wes, still apparently preoccupied by his mother's condition, made no response.

The rest of the day, with the dinner-on-the ground, the afternoon singing fest, and the evening service, was buoyed along by a shared and often expressed feeling that the revival had gotten off to a good start. The Miller boys' confession had helped to put everyone in the right spirit, and Miss Hattie's presence added a tantalizing element, as she herself seemed totally aware, joining in the singing with loud, sure tones, showing by not looking once at a proffered hymnal that she felt completely at home, even if she *was* a Baptist.

On Monday, Mr. Walter went to open up the drugstore, and then he took the day off to drive Brother Billy around on visits. Sunday conversations, added to the Gaffords' words of advice, provided directions as to the objects of these visits. Brother Billy read from his Bible and said a prayer in the parlors of two or three who were troubled or who had been missing services. (Everybody told everybody else that Brother Billy could be counted on to say the "sweetest prayers.") They sat briefly on the front porches of some who had been labeled prime prospects: "fine folks but alien sinners who never darken the doors of any church."

They purposely deferred until the last a visit in the home of Sister Georgia Darden, for they wanted her husband to be home from work before they arrived. Sure enough, he was there, his face glowing pinkly and his hair still wet from a dousing. They thanked him for coming to church on Sunday morning and hoped he would support all of the services, along with Miss Georgia. She sat on the squeaking swing beside her husband, clearly tense and anxiously listening for his response. What he answered was civil, but terse and non-committal. She looked disappointed, though she knew this was the way it turned out every year: he went with her the first day of the revival because she begged him so hard, and that was the end of it for another year. She had hoped that maybe this time Brother Billy would be a bit firmer, but instead he smiled softly and talked on as if he believed her husband would be on the front pew that very night.

Everybody reminded everybody else that Monday night was the poorest one for attendance and that they must not become discouraged by a small crowd.

"We're few in numbers, Brothers and Sisters," said Brother Foster as he announced the first song: "but we're big in spirit, and 'where two or three are gathered together,' you know. So sing out loud and from the heart."

Brother Billy preached as earnestly as he would have to a thousand. He felt a twinge of disappointment when there were no responses during the singing of the invitation song, but as he looked into the faces lifted toward him, with mouths wide in song, he told himself with gladness that they, like him, were thankful recipients of that "Blessed Assurance."

On the next day, Tuesday, Brother Billy rode into Shiloh with Mr. Walter, planning to pick up a few items and then to visit around on the square until noon. But his stops at the several business establishments went faster than he had anticipated, so he stuck his head into the open door of the drugstore to tell Mr. Walter that he had decided to walk on back to the house and get a little extra studying done.

He was about halfway there, walking slowly along and savoring the sounds and smells of nature, when a car came up behind him, throwing gravel as it screeched to a stop just even with him.

He turned, smiling a greeting, expecting to look into a familiar face. But this was a person he had never met. The total picture was a shocking disruption to the serene pastoral setting. Looking at him through her opened window was a woman that struck him as being in her middle thirties except for her brown eyes with reddish flecks. They belonged to an ancient, world-weary soul. Her hair was in amazing bright-red ringlets, and her lips and earrings were red too. She took him in with a steady gaze that would have penetrated any facade. She seemed amused at his expression or at what she saw beneath it, for her lips were obviously fighting with a smile.

"I know you. You're the famous preacher boy." The rough, yet furry depth of her voice came as such a surprise to him that he found it difficult to respond.

"Yes, ma'am, I'm Billy Rucker. I don't believe we've met." This was as near to social hypocrisy as his open nature had ever been, for he was completely certain that he had never been near anyone remotely like her, and his mind spun in an attempt to imagine who she might be. At the same time, strangely, there came into his mind the strident voices of his fellow students delving into the enigmas awaiting those who would be "soul doctors."

"No, we've not met—that's a fact." That voice again. "I'm Lottie Lee Simpson. Miz Warren's daughter." Her voice rose oddly at the end, giving the assertion the effect of a question.

"Of course, I knew Sister Warren. They told me she passed away last winter, bless her soul. But she was a brave little martyr, suffering so long with that crippling arthritis and all." There was a sense of relief in being able to attach to this strange young woman an identity and safely put her in her rightful place, but his forehead creased as he thought back.

"I don't believe I knew that she had a daughter, though."

"Yeah. Well, she wasn't exactly proud enough to advertise, I guess. Anyhow, I come back when she died, and I've been staying at the home place. Temporary."

"I see," said Brother Billy, only partly enlightened but unsure as to whether he ought to seek further. He laid his hand on the warm top of the little green coupe, still at a loss as to what to say to this dramatic-looking stranger.

"I know you're staying with the Gaffords. Get in here if you're brave enough." She laughed, not as if she were amused at all now, but rather as if embarrassed at her own daring in offering *a preacher* a ride.

"Thanks a lot. It *is* getting warm." He folded himself into the small space and slammed the door, then looked straight ahead with an unaccustomed uneasiness which he could not exactly define.

They rode in silence down the gravel road, with the sound of the motor and the tires creating a thin shield between them, preventing an unbearable confrontation. Eventually he furtively studied her out of the corner of his eye. Her lashes, heavy with mascara, hid her eyes from him entirely; they seemed one mesh of blackness as she squinted against the mid-morning sun. Her shoulders were brown and bare and warm looking; they were dotted with reddish brown freckles swarming down her arms and onto the backs of her hands. Her sun dress was of a soft white jersey-like material that outlined her thighs and stopped above her knees. Freckles like those on her arms shone through her sheer hose where they stretched across her bent knee near his. He adjusted the sun visor and peered ahead.

"I hope we'll see you at church, Sister. . . ."

She laughed, a hard little syllable of a laugh, and as she turned her head to throw a glance at him, the smell of smoke blended with the heavy perfume that filled the interior of the car.

"Better call me Lottie Lee," she chuckled, pulling to the edge of the road beside the Gafford mailbox. "I don't think our holy Christians would want to claim me as their sister. Take her, for instance."

She nodded toward the house, and he turned in time to see a slight movement of the lace curtains on Miss Lizzie's big picture window.

"See, Brother . . . Billy Boy,"—a look dared him to think her too forward—"I'm everything Shiloh hates, all tied up in one bundle."

She leaned forward, mashing her bosom against the rim of the steering wheel, and the blood-red tips of her fingers flashed as she clasped and unclasped her hands on the top of the wheel.

"Why, Lottie Lee? What do you mean?" He asked her reluctantly, half hoping she would refuse to say more, leaving him with his clouded understanding, his superficial, still safe concern.

"Well, I dye my hair." Ruefully, she stretched one of the ringlets above her ear to its full length and then turned it loose to allow it to spring back into place.

"Second," she went on, as if she were presenting the points of a Sunday school lesson to a slow pupil, "I smoke." With that she flapped a hand in the direction of a nearly empty cigarette pack on the top of the dashboard. He looked at it and at its distorted reflection in the windshield.

"And—get ready—I am *divorced!*" Suddenly she slapped him on the arm and cackled at his astonishment, tossing back her head so that he could see the pink inside her mouth.

About that time Mr. Walter's car came up behind them—he wasn't sure if it had been there a moment before he came to himself enough to notice—and turned fast into the driveway. He leaped out, slammed his door, and headed toward the back of the house with only the briefest of glances toward Lottie Lee's car. The lace panels on the front window eased together.

"You'd better get out of here before you get all contaminated." She laughed again, that same hard little fragment, like a piece of broken glass, shifting in the seat and not looking straight at him.

When he had closed the door, he leaned down to look back at her through the open window. His voice was tight and unfamiliar sounding to his own ears when he spoke her name.

"Lottie Lee."

The brass had all disappeared when at last she returned his earnest gaze from lost eyes that seemed to him deep wells into which he was being sucked until he must surely drown.

"Please come tonight," he said huskily and then turned and walked quickly toward the house, aware in his bones more than his ears of the sound of the car's gear changing and of the wheels spinning in loose gravel as she took off fast. As he angled toward the little side stoop with its door opening into the guest room, he could see the taillights glowing as she slowed to turn right onto the Warren lane.

He didn't see the Gaffords until five o'clock. They did not expect him to join them for lunch since he did not ordinarily do so when they were invited to a big dinner preceding evening services. He took out his prepared sermon notes and went over them until he had to face the fact that he found them distasteful and somehow irrelevant. For the first time, the soothing assertions, the easy answers which had heretofore risen from an undisturbed soul—a soul which repudiated eddies and ripples and waves to threaten the faithful—stuck in his throat and clogged his nostrils until he felt unable to breathe.

Then he removed his shoes and, in sock feet, stretched out on the bed, his eyes shut and his hands nervously clutching the Bible which rested on his chest.

Finally, feeling panic invading the room and his very being, he abruptly rose from the bed and went to sit in a stuffed chair by the window, placed there by Miss Lizzie for his convenience. He turned to the Gospel of John and alternately read, rubbed his hand into the aching sockets of his eyes, and stared out the window, only dimly seeing the green field and a hay baler moving methodically in and out of the scope of his vision.

By five o'clock, when he left his room dressed for church and climbed into the car with the Gaffords, he was so completely given over to the grip of tension that he had trouble focusing. There was little talk as they sped along, the two men in the front and Miss Lizzie in the back with half the seat taken up by her big straw hat, ready to be put on after supper.

The Burgesses were ready to welcome them, along with the song director and his wife, and a few visiting relatives from out-lying communities. The preacher and the Gaffords completed the assembly, the latter regularly included at the nightly feasts because of their functions as hosts and chauffeur to the visiting preacher.

Brother Billy mechanically engaged in conversation during the meal, aware of an uneasiness that he could not shake, an uneasiness that was infinitely more disturbing because it was inexplicable and, for him, unprecedented. He was awkwardly self-conscious, certain that his face could be easily read by any who cared to glance.

Hardly anybody at church seemed to notice when Lottie Lee came in at the last moment before starting time and eased into the back pew, behind a row of whispering teenagers. Brother Billy himself was not aware of her presence until he stood to begin his sermon and, scanning the audience, caught her eye, timid and frightened. Losing his poise, he stumbled through his introduc-tory remarks. He shuffled the pages of his notes to give himself time to breathe deeply.

Recovering sufficiently to go on with relative calm, he began to discuss the theme of Living Water. Miss Lizzie was removing her fan from her purse and unfolding it. Her expression as she looked at him was cool but unreadable.

"Some of you dear souls who live on your farms outside Shiloh know how precious good water is. And some of you know how tedious it is to carry it in buckets from those cold springs to your houses. Sister Powers knows." He turned in her direction, and she nodded back, glowing under everybody's gaze.

He postponed getting to his point. "And, Brothers and Sisters, the blessed Holley family know how to value the gift of good water."

Bodies shifted and heads turned so that everyone could see the Holley family, filling a whole pew with five children forming stair steps. Beaming self-consciously, they squirmed while the congregation briefly looked at them. Then, looks moved two pews farther back, where Lottie Lee sat, marble-white and frightened. As if by signal all turned to face the front, but an undercurrent continued. Somehow, Brother Billy thought, he must find a way to bring the congregation back to itself.

Taking up his Bible, he began to read loudly and emotionally the text that he could easily have quoted from memory. Then, discussing the exchange between Jesus and the Woman at the Well, he studiously avoided the back of the room as well as the front, where Miss Lizzie had given up fanning and was sitting as though stunned. He addressed the air above the disturbed blanket of faces.

"And should we condemn that woman, that soul who thirsted to be what she was not—who thirsted for the *truth?*"

He glanced at the congregation as he sensed a change in demeanor. Several, who ordinarily settled into a comfortable doze after the first few minutes, sat wide awake, obviously surprised by his fervor, and by the hesitancy with which he spoke: some words crept forth, followed by the tumbling out of entire phrases. Fascinated gazes followed his unconscious gestures which were spontaneous rather than ornaments of training and practice.

Miss Mamie Wall, in the second pew with her niece, was too deaf to know how loudly she said, "My lands, he's turning into a Holy Roller!"

Brother Billy laid his outline on the side of the lectern. His voice trembled as he spoke of the awful, gripping power of temptation, the reality of sin, and the need for help in fighting the forces of darkness.

"My brothers and sisters, should we despise the woman who talked with our Lord at the well? I should say not! Rather, pity her for bearing the shame. Admire her for facing the wreck of her poor life. And praise her heroism as she risked all to bring others to the Lord! Just imagine the crowds that ridiculed her, accused her, then listened to her and followed her to the place where He waited!"

At last he let his eyes fall to where Lottie Lee sat, her eyes like great black pools, like the eyes of a cornered doe. Her eyes did not leave his face, and her countenance showed that for her, as for him, there were only the two of them in the room.

By the time the invitation song was announced, Miss Lizzie had put her fan back into her purse, and her lips were one thin line. When the congregation stood while sinners were invited to come, she clutched at Mr. Walter's arm as if the strength to stand had left her. He held the hymnal for her to see, but not a word could she bring herself to sing.

When the plaintive hymn droned to a close, Brother Billy found himself beside the fourth pew. The wood which he clutched was damp. He blindly moved to the front, feeling questioning eyes puncture his back.

At the sound of "amen," he rushed toward the back of the auditorium, ignoring the few extended hands that brushed his sleeve. Before he could reach Lottie Lee, she had pushed her way into the aisle behind several who had passed her without a look. Brother Billy saw two red circles disappearing around a curve when he reached the steps.

The ride home with the Gaffords was practically silent, with only a brief exchange or two between the husband and wife. The interior of the car teemed with thoughts palpable though unexpressed. In the driveway, Brother Billy murmured a terse "good night" and, instead of entering the house, began to walk down the dark road. The Gaffords looked at each other in disbelief before going through the back door and turning off the outside light, leaving the lawn dark under thick foliage.

It was on the next day and the days immediately following that Mr. Tucker, who regularly left home at 2 A.M. to pick up daily papers to deliver, had the opportunity to share some surprising facts. He related how he had noticed lights—or a light—glaring in the old Warren place, which he had to pass on the way into Shiloh. At the time, he said, he only vaguely wondered if maybe that daughter of Mrs. Warren had taken sick or something. Later, of course, things became clear and everything fitted together, but on the night itself, it was left to the Gaffords alone to know just how much was amiss.

The next morning when Brother Billy entered the breakfast nook, Mr. Walter was leaning against the counter while talking on the phone. He ended the conversation abruptly and briefly greeted Brother Billy without looking directly at him. Miss Lizzie's lips were stretched even thinner than they had been the night before, and her heavy silence was extraordinary.

Having looked around for his keys and located them on the dinette table, Mr. Walter, studying the tiled floor as if he expected to find a message for him there, cleared his throat twice before speaking.

"Been talking with some of the other brethren this morning, uh. . . . Seems like they feel—and I can go along with their thinking—that, well, in this day and time, a long revival is just a little too hard on busy country folks like most of us are here and around Shiloh. We're figuring that Brother Rudolph will be back from his sick leave about September, and he can start off with a little pep-up week-end revival. Maybe so."

He had to stop and clear his throat again, still looking every way but at Brother Billy. "So, I've made out your check—like they asked me to—" He fumbled in his coat pocket and brought out the folded check. Rather than hand it to Brother Billy, he laid it on the counter beside the sugar bowl.

"Hurry up, Lizzie, you'll make us both late," he shouted over his shoulder. At last he turned in the general direction of Brother Billy, who sat at the narrow table periodically taking sips of warm coffee without the least awareness that he was doing so.

"My wife has a beauty parlor appointment, and I need to head down to the store. Now you just take your time and get your things together, and I'll be back in plenty of time to get you to your bus." He spoke formally and precisely as to a perfect stranger.

Miss Lizzie sailed through the room with her purse and a lumpy crochet bag, and the two rushed out the back door without a glance or a word to Brother Billy.

He sat for several more minutes at the table, as if stunned. Finally he pushed his cup distastefully from him and scraped his chair away from the table.

There was a telephone book on the counter, and he was soon able to find the number he wanted. He rang once to rouse the operator.

"Good morning, Sister Betty."

She immediately recognized his voice, and they exchanged a few pleasantries. As she complimented him on his sermons and seemed likely to go on for some time, Brother Billy fought to control his impatience.

"Sister Betty," he finally broke in, "will you please connect me with 25-J?"

Instantly a heavy silence hummed across the line into his ear, and then some loud pops told him that she was ringing the number.

It was a little later that Miss Lizzie saw Brother Billy for the last time. Her head had evolved into a mass of pinned and rolled knots, and she was being turned to deeper and deeper shades of pink under the dryer nearest the window when she happened to glance up from her crocheting.

Changing from pink to purple even as she stared, she pushed the dryer up and stood so fast she dislodged a front roller, which bounced on the linoleum at her feet.

"Pearl, honey, let me use that phone," she said breathlessly.

When Betty connected her with the drug store phone and the clerk called her husband to the front, she cupped a hand around her mouth so that Pearl and the other customers couldn't hear the shameful thing she had to tell him.

"It's a wonder I hadn't had a stroke right here, with my hair rolled up," she declared into the mouth of the receiver. "Just innocently look out the window and what do I see? Him right there in the front seat with that henna-headed hussy driving right down the middle of Main Street. I say good riddance, but, oh, the embarrassment if people find out. I mean outsiders and all." A few short exchanges punctuated by violent nods and shakes of her head, and she hung up the receiver so hard that it tinkled.

She reached for a magazine to fan herself and then, before sitting down, rang the phone once to get the operator back.

"Betty Lou, precious, I thought I would explain what that was about in case you got the tail end of it. . . ."

After Betty had contributed her personal knowledge pertaining to the episode—that is, the shocking fact of the early morning telephone call—Miss Lizzie let her go and asked Pearl to feel her hair to see if it was dry. Since it was, she crawled up into a chair to be combed out. By now the other ladies, except for one who was slouched over in a beet-colored sleep, had turned their dryers off and were waiting, staring hungrily at Miss Lizzie's reflection.

"Pearl, honey, I'm sorry you had to hear, because it certainly makes the church look bad, but you might as well hear the balance of it now."

When she had finished, everybody said they were flabbergasted about Brother Billy's part in the sordid affair, but no one was a bit surprised about Lottie Lee.

"I taught that young she-scamp in the third grade," supplied one of the ladies leaning forward from her dryer chair, her eyes sparkling. "I hate to say it, but she was simply a bad seed. You don't have to wait till they're grown to find that out. Of course, she didn't have a chance, in spite of her poor old mother. Her father, you know." She raised well plucked brows. "And he had a sister turned out just this same way." She clicked her teeth and absent-mindedly turned the pages of a magazine while her mind was obviously reviewing episodes from Lottie Lee's wild life.

"Her poor mama did try, though," sighed the other customer.

"I suppose," said Miss Lizzie with the hint of some doubt, and she leaned toward the mirror to check the tint of her hair.

"Pearl, dear, I appreciate the way you keep my hair looking perfectly natural."

Pearl patted her on the shoulder and continued combing, periodically stopping and turning her head to one side to admire her handiwork in the mirror.

"Well," she said, "I do good to go to my own church, staying on my feet all day long the way I do. But from what I've heard, that Rucker fellow must have had everybody fooled."

Miss Lizzie stretched her lips. "I tried to think the best, the way I always do. But—I don't remember if I ever hinted this to any of you girls"—she glanced at the rapt images in the mirror—"but I saw this *streak* in him from the start. I hoped he'd overcome it, I really did." She sighed. "But when the streak's there, you'd better watch out!"

"I wonder," mused the school teacher, "if going to that seminary did it. They tell me that most of their teachers are admitted atheists, and—."

Miss Lizzie shook her head right out from under Pearl's hands. "I saw it before he even went to any seminary. I tell you, the streak was there, just waiting for some Lottie Lee to come prissing up. I just pray that it'll turn out for the best and that it doesn't harm the good work of the church too much."

"I know what you mean" agreed Pearl.

The other ladies nodded.

Hiding behind Veils

The Long View

he narrow country road that would take us past the old
Wills farm began to wind through a thick pine forest where
naked trunks reached high before sending out limbs to meet and
entwine above the near darkness they had created. By the time
we reached the edge of the dense forest and wound out into full
sunshine, the glare was an intrusion upon our eyes.

The route was as familiar to my parents and me as the tale of
the tragedy that had befallen Miss DeeLee so long ago. I could
drive without having to think, knowing when to slow down for
a bump or an extreme curve. I also knew, on a level beyond
thought, that as we felt ourselves being brought ever nearer to
the old house, the three of us in a very real sense became separated from each other in worlds furnished with questions and
images which could not be shared. Between Papa and me in the
front seat, and between us and Mama, leaning forward to peer
over Papa's shoulder and out his open window, a familiar but
ever-strange gulf surged, one too deep to be plumbed or spanned.
Each of us had to try one more time to come to terms with an
event that had ripped at the delicate fabric of our security and
even our beliefs in self-knowledge.

When it happened, and for years afterward, I had blamed
them for shutting me out, for keeping from me the solution to

mysteries that would not turn me loose and let me move on. They evaded the questions I asked and seemed oblivious to those that gnawed and gnawed and went unvoiced. It was easier to believe that they had deliberately slammed a door between me and the knowledge I sought than to face the possibility that they, the wisest and best and the ones with whom I shared the greatest love and understanding, did not themselves have the answers. They were, therefore, the most guilty participants in a plot to keep me from knowing the truth about Miss DeeLee's death—which meant the truth about her *life*—and, for some incredible reason, *my* life.

Then my anger continued to smolder at their apparent ability, along with everybody else except me, to forget her, to leave what had happened to her comfortably in the past, and to go on as if she had never lived and loved and wept and died. I think I must have drawn strength from the righteous indignation that wrapped about me.

While it still smarted like a personal affront—for indeed it was that—to realize that it was mostly as if Miss DeeLee and her Mr. Albert had never been, I had at least learned, in the process of my own growing up, that Mama and Papa, like me, had had to look for ways to cope with spots of darkness and to impose some semblance of order upon what threatened to lead to chaos and to madness.

Papa's way was to reach back with his mind to the times before the ruin set in, to the good times. His smooth, carefully selected words were fitted together to make a wall. Before he began to speak, I knew that Mama, like me, could hear the gentle whirring and grinding of his mental machinery which would produce, by and by, the long, familiar flow of Wills-related memories spiced with anecdotes gleaned from many occasions when he had gone to Long View to preach. He always concluded with nostalgic accounts of the singings and dinners on the ground— the finest to be enjoyed anywhere in Alabama and Tennessee. I used to think of Miss DeeLee and her contributions to these events and be almost sickened at Papa's callous gusto.

Mama, riding along quietly and letting the wind ruffle her short, gray hair, sighed at this point, but not in the way she did when her patience was wearing thin. Her own memories of the Willses and of Long View went back to her childhood, and I knew that her secret thoughts were taking Papa's words as a kind of outline for which she supplied her own development.

The powerful connection which I had felt to Miss DeeLee through the years was something even I could not come near to explaining. How could she, a mature woman, and I, a nondescript child, one of a swarm of children usually chasing each other in rowdy play, have *known* each other? But from my first memory I had held her as special and had embroidered my perception of her reality with a vivid and active imagination. A few times she had looked at me as if she really saw me there, and once, when her frustrating veil was removed and folded away, we had actually looked into each other's eyes, and in the dark brightness of hers I had seen myself reflected.

To Weegie she was a curiosity barely making a ripple in the smooth waters of her uncomplicated existence. To my parents, before it happened, she must have been far too familiar to be other than taken for granted. But to me she represented doors and rooms of doors that lured and challenged me outside myself and then into myself.

So, after she was no longer there, I continued, because I had to, to ponder her nature and her motives and to speculate on their meaning with respect to me. I must search for the *real* Miss DeeLee that nobody else knew or even suspected to exist. My quest, rather than fading out, became more crucial as I began to evolve from a lonely sensitive child into a young woman facing the frightening task of finding or making a self with whom it might be possible to live in some peace. Sometimes, in a stressful moment when I felt that I was bound to weep or burst before closed doors and the mysteries whose answers were barred from me, it seemed that the tears were for Miss DeeLee and myself at the same time—that the poor dead lady and I merged into one person by virtue of our being washed in the same warm tears. If she became a fixation, so be it; she deserved an interpreter, and I believed that I was meant to fill that role.

Obviously, there were layers of truth to be known about her that even a precocious child—and I was not that—could not have guessed. After all, I was only nine years old when she died, and the most deeply etched image was that of a stern, starched, formidable lady with a voice that bore a sharpness, at least to the ears of an awe-struck child, even when she was saying something kind. Still, I was drawn to her by a special fascination at the same time that something held me at a distance.

My sister Weegie, three years younger than I, was in no way inhibited by awe or a budding sense of propriety, and she unwittingly became an instrument in sparking my imaginative involvement in Miss DeeLee's secret self, burgeoning with a life beyond ordinariness. She would have been five, going on six, on that sleepy Sunday which I especially remember, for it was in the spring preceding the August when the terrible deed was done.

Miss DeeLee had invited us to come home with her and Mr. Albert for dinner. Since Weegie and I were the only children present on this occasion, we were permitted to sit at the dining table, along with the adults, rather than to take plates loaded by Mama and go to the back porch. Besides my family, there was a Brother Austin from Birmingham, who got invited at the last minute because he was a stranger and a visitor to Long View. He and the Willses said how good Papa's sermon was, and Papa and Mama said how delicious the food was, and everything was just the way it always was. I pushed a pickled peach around on my plate and wondered whether I dared take both chicken and ham.

After a while, Papa laid down his fork and leaned back to rest and pat his chin with his napkin. Right away I knew that he was about to remember something.

"Sister Wills," he said, "when I think of you, I always get a picture of those big baskets of food you bring to every single Long View dinner-on-the-ground. Brother Austin, you've missed something. Always covered with the whitest cloth that ever blinded a man's eye, and not one drop of grease or anything else to give a hint of what's inside that basket."

Miss DeeLee stood up to help with passing bowls and platters and make sure Papa got the full benefits of the other side of the table too. I tried to be extra careful of the tablecloth.

After dinner the men took straight chairs out under one of the pine trees in the front yard. Mama and I helped Miss DeeLee carry part of the food to the icebox on the back porch, while Weegie held the screen door open for us and shooed flies. Then Miss DeeLee spread another big white cloth over the table with the rest of the food and the dishes still on, creating mysterious little points and mounds and valleys. Miss DeeLee said we would go sit on the front porch where it would be cooler.

A low bench without a back stood against the wall, and I sat on it. Mama took the rocker and immediately began to work on her tatting, which she always wadded into her purse on Sunday morning for use in whiling away the long afternoon hours. Miss DeeLee sat straight and still in a corner of the swing. The shade cast by thick wisteria made part of her dress look dark purple, while the rest of it, I thought, was almost the color of the clusters of blooms that hung among the black-green leaves.

Mama and Miss DeeLee talked with long pauses mixed in with words. There were no interesting topics, so I watched the variegated lace grow longer and make a pretty, snake-like pattern against Mama's light blue dress. From a few feet away the men's words merged into a sleep-inducing drone. Insects buzzed in the vines and added their contribution to the heaviness that was an expected part of Sunday, spent away from one's own books and toys.

Then the men decided to walk through the pasture back of the house and on to the corn and cotton fields beyond, to check on Mr. Albert's prospects. Weegie, who had been entertaining herself by pestering an old dog who was trying to snooze at Mr. Albert's feet, leaped up to follow them. She went into a sulk when Mama told her to take a seat on the porch. She deliberately postponed complete obedience by stooping in front of Mama and playing with the tail of lace that was by then spiraling to the floor. When Mama had had enough, she spoke sharply and told her to sit beside her sister.

Instead, she marched over to the swing and plopped down beside Miss DeeLee, making the chains creak and cry a little. She spread her skirt beside Miss DeeLee's. When she started to speak, she was trying to use her adult-conversation voice, specifically Papa's.

"Sister Wills," she began, "where are *your* children?"

Weegie knew better than to ask questions as well as I did, but when Mama looked up from the work in her lap, Weegie's blue eyes stared right back into Mama's that were just like them, and then she coolly turned to Miss DeeLee to wait for an answer.

Miss DeeLee didn't sound like herself when she finally began to speak. Her voice was lower and softer. I listened hard, for I desperately wanted to know, though I would never have asked.

"Darling, Mr. Albert and I only had one child. Dear little Percy Albert went away from us when he was a wee bit of a boy."

"Where did he go to?" Weegie asked, looking up into Miss DeeLee's face with great curiosity.

"Now, Weegie, that's enough," Mama said, but Miss DeeLee went on.

"We laid him to rest right up in the Long View Cemetery, along with the Davises, honey," she said, gazing way off as if she could see it plain from where she sat.

Miss DeeLee didn't know we were staring at her, for her eyes were too sad and busy trying to pick out one particular thing.

Of course, she wasn't wearing her veil, and I was as always fascinated to see her eyes and to wonder what she was seeing. At church she never failed to wear a brimmed black hat—straw in summer and soft felt in winter—draped with a thick veil that reached down to her chin and puffed gently outward when she talked and even more when she sang. But when we were invited home with her, she would first seat us in the front room on the white wicker furniture that would leave checked prints on the backs of our legs. Then she would excuse herself and go into another room, and when she came back, there would be her long-ish face with its sharp black eyes and her iron gray hair pulled back tightly into a huge club that made me speculate about what it would look like loosed and hanging down her back. I supposed Mr. Albert had seen it that way. I wondered, though, if even he could tell what her eyes were looking for. Sometimes when she looked at me and asked a question, I failed to answer because she seemed to be looking all the way through me at someone else. I was confused, too, by a strange embarrassment, as if looking at her naked face were somehow wrong or intrusive.

But I had never seen her looking as far as she did after Weegie's question. The next thing, Weegie leaned over, close to Miss DeeLee, and began to finger the pin that was always at the neck of her dress. The black profile of an old-fashioned lady stuck out from a white background.

"Child, my Granny Davis gave me that before Mr. Albert and I were married."

"Is it a picture of your granny?" Weegie asked.

"Goodness, no, child, it's just a cameo," she softly replied, and she looked straight at me.

Weegie moved back into her corner of the swing. "It's pretty," she said politely, glancing at Mama to estimate from tautness of her lips the degree to which she had overstepped the boundary of safety.

I don't remember whether Weegie was chastised or punished, for soon after that, all of my memories of the Willses and of normal times were smeared and blurred by blackness and blood. The predictable that I had counted on without knowing it had been snatched away, and nothing was the same after that.

It was only a few weeks later, when the weather was just beginning to be like real summer, that Mr. Albert died. I heard all about that, for the adults talked about it for weeks. He had taken a long time coming back from the orchard, where he had gone with a tin pan to pick up some fallen June apples. Miss DeeLee got to wondering about his delay, so she put on his old shirt that she wore when she was outside, to keep from getting brown and freckled. She walked out the back of the house and through the pasture, expecting any minute to meet him on his way back.

She found him lying a few yards from the squatty old apple trees, flat on his back with the pan upturned and a dozen or so apples scattered about in the grass. She shook him and called his name, but he only looked at her out of clouded eyes and soundlessly moved lips that were twisted to one side of his face.

She must have flown back to the house then, for Mr. Tucker, the mail carrier, said that he heard her screaming just as he was putting the weekly paper into the box and slamming the lid. Then he noticed this streak that turned out to be Mr. Albert's old Sunday shirt on Miss DeeLee just flying around the corner of the front porch. By the time she got to him, he had already jumped out of his car and locked the door. He couldn't make out a word she was saying except "Albert" and "orchard" over and over as she tugged violently at his arm with both of her hands. He followed her, stopping at the corner of the back yard to clang the dinner bell several times and to scrawl "orchard" on a penny postcard he found in his pocket and leave it on top of a tub beside the bell post.

Some men from a nearby hayfield were the first to get down there, and Mr. Ross from just up the road and his twelve-yearold grandson hobbling with bare feet over the sharp stubble. Mr. Albert was already gone, though, before the Rosses arrived. The men picked him up and started back to the house. Mr. Tucker practically had to carry Miss DeeLee too, moaning and holding to her bosom the pan she had picked up out of the weeds.

By the time they reached the house, the neighbor ladies were there, and they took charge of Miss DeeLee while one of the men went home to call somebody about Mr. Albert's body.

Mr. Tucker finished his mail route in a hurry and called Papa from the Shiloh Post Office to tell him what had happened. Mama turned the stove off from under the bean pot, and we all piled into the car immediately, with Weegie and me in the back seat trying to make something of the unsatisfactory answers to our questions.

Once there, we moved through a group of low-talking men and a few round-eyed children standing around in the shade. Mama whispered that we would wait on the front porch while Papa went in first. He closed the screen door behind him without allowing it to pop and stepped inside where it was dark except next to the door and the windows. At first there was loud crying and talking at the same time, and then only moanings and Papa's voice that made one stream of soft sounds without breaking into separate words. It was as if everybody in there was behind Miss DeeLee's veil. We didn't dare mash our faces against the screen wire, so all we could see was the hazy outline of Miss DeeLee in the corner and Papa in a straight chair close beside her. Somebody else was in the big rocker, making it go back and forth steadily, but I couldn't see well enough to guess who that might be.

Papa came out and said something low to Mama about clothes. We followed her when she went in and hugged Miss DeeLee. They cried together for a while. Miss DeeLee seemed to me to be more remote than ever before; I did not feel that she would know me if she looked straight at me. Weegie and I huddled behind Mama's skirts, and at first my eyes were too full of the outside light to take anything in.

Then the person in the rocker said, "How're you gulls," and I saw that it was Miss Lottie from the Mercantile, with her big beads and patches of white powder on her face and neck. She was fanning with the fan she could fold up and carry in her purse. When it was open and not moving too fast, you could see palm trees and brown people in long robes. But in this room it was one moving blur.

Then Mama went into Miss DeeLee's bedroom with us following, afraid to be left behind in the strangeness. Miss DeeLee seemed like a visitor from some faraway place, sitting there trying different ways to fold her hands.

It seemed odd and dreamlike to be in her bedroom with Mama opening up her bureau drawers and touching her private things. When she opened one drawer, the whole room was filled with the smell of too many sweet flowers. Mama lifted out a tiny yellowed baby dress and then put it back and closed the drawer. Finally she came to a drawer that poured forth the aroma of cloved apples such as I had smelled when Grandma Esther opened an old trunk in her attic. Now Mama took out folded white things and laid them on the bed. Next she opened the closet door and pulled out Mr. Albert's black suit on a padded hanger that made the shoulders stand out fuller and taller than Mr. Albert ever did. We tiptoed behind her as she went the back way, through the narrow hall, through the kitchen, and around the house to where Papa was standing with the other men. Mr. Tucker was back, and everybody was listening to him tell all about it again, letting it be *his* story. He pointed and shook his head and now and then took off his flat-billed cap to scratch his head and fan a little.

Mama handed Papa the clothes to carry into town to the Undertaker, and Weegie and I went with him while Mama went back inside to be with Miss DeeLee.

Somehow I managed not to think of Mr. Albert much, except in connection with Miss DeeLee. I never had. After that day, in the dark room, I didn't see her without her veil on, and I was left with a really burning desire to know what her grieving face looked like under its concealing cover. I felt that if I could see her dark eyes, and they could look at me and see my sympathy, she would be helped. I pictured her lips trembling and tears rolling down her cheeks, and I imagined that I was able to share her sorrow.

Once, on a weekday, we passed her house on the way to Grandma Esther's, and she was sitting on her front porch, just sitting there with her hands folded. I could not see the features of her face, much less her expression. She looked altogether like an old-fashioned portrait, ready, except for a frame, to be hung in someone's gray, damp-smelling parlor. In the swing was the short, fat lady with pink hair who had come over from Mississippi to attend the funeral and stay a few weeks with Miss DeeLee. I heard her telling her name to people at church. "Ah'm DeeLee's Cud'nellie," she drawled, and I never knew whether she was Cousin Ellie or Cousin Nellie, but it didn't make any difference.

I closely scrutinized Miss DeeLee at church, staring at her black, shining back and perceiving now and then a gentle shaking. I felt sure she was weeping, in the strange, silent way that adults have, and I longed to invade and share her thoughts. While dry flies sawed the air outside the open windows and Papa stood in the pulpit saying the beautiful words that I was convinced would make everybody good who sat beneath their flow, I watched Miss DeeLee and heard every utterance as I believed she was hearing it. I wondered whether she had difficulty with recalling what Mr. Albert had looked like, as I did. I pictured her, after Cud'nellie had gone to bed, opening up the special drawer and touching little Percy Albert's baby things. When once she passed me in the aisle, she laid a gloved hand on my shoulder, and the place she touched burned as if her hurt had been transferred to me in a special way.

As always, the approach of August and the big homecoming aroused constant excitement throughout the whole neighborhood. On the Saturday before the long-awaited event, an all-day working at Long View ended with the windows all scrubbed, the floors polished to a high shine, and every blade of grass and

weed trimmed or uprooted around the building and in the graveyard. Almost everyone was expecting company, either relatives
or former neighbors who had moved to distant parts but were
always faithful to head toward Long View in August.

On the day itself we were a little late in leaving home because
of the special preparations. For once—and the bitterness of this
did not escape me for a moment—I didn't even think to look
toward the Wills house as we passed, simply because I was intent
upon balancing on my knees the heavy rectangular chocolate
cake that Mama had gotten up early to bake so that it would still
be warm and fresh. Weegie kept putting her legs against a big
bag of ice wrapped in newspapers and fitted into the floorboard
on her side, screaming that she couldn't stand its coldness. Papa
was always quiet on the way to church, as if he were going over
his sermon one more time in his mind.

We had a longer wait between Sunday school and the preaching service on Homecoming Day, for this was the time when
most of the visitors flocked in, hugging and kissing with juicy
smacks, and getting so loud in their greetings that I was afraid
they would never be able to hush and let Papa preach.

It was during this interim that somebody missed Miss DeeLee.
Mr. Ross offered to run back up the road in his truck to see if
maybe the Mississippi cousin had gone home and Miss DeeLee
didn't have a way to get there with her big basket.

Papa was standing by the front pew and most people were
sitting down and talking in lower tones when Mr. Ross returned.
He caught Papa's eye and motioned for him to come back to the
door, where several of the men who had been loitering outside
until the last minute were now clustered together with funny
looks on their faces. Then they all left and Papa came back down
front for services to begin.

I had thought Mr. Ross looked white, and Papa was pale
too as he stood up to welcome all the visitors and to deliver his
special Homecoming Day sermon. His voice trembled in places,

but it did that sometimes. The ladies, especially, thought it sounded "sweet" and "sincere," and they were always telling him so.

The minute the last amen was said, noisy greetings and laughter erupted again, and in the aisle the ladies were pushing to get outside to spread the goodies waiting in baskets and boxes in their cars or on the white-draped trestles under the nearby pines, on the side of the building opposite the graveyard.

But Papa didn't stand and shake hands as he usually did. Once outside, he found Mama and, after a whispered conversation with her and Grandma Esther, got into the car and backed out of the lot fast, making dust fog up from the road. Some lady reaching into the trunk of her car hollered at him, and he answered that he certainly would take a helping of every single dish when he returned.

Grandma Esther merely told Weegie and me that our parents had to go somewhere and would probably be back soon. But before everybody had piled up a paper plate the first time, the talk was going around that Miss DeeLee Wills was *dead*. People would talk loud, and then they would put their heads close together and say things I couldn't hear. I gathered, though, that she had *wanted* to die; and I thought of her again, as I had so often pictured her, missing her dead baby boy and Mr. Albert so much that her spirit just finally tore loose from her body and flew off to find them. That's what I thought they must mean, and the fact of her being gone from us forever was too unreal for me to comprehend it, not then and not for a long time to come.

Those were strange times, the days that followed, when I felt shut out, left alone to tug at a mystery that I couldn't identify or even prove to exist. Miss DeeLee's death was the only reality of which I was certain. Mama was sick, and we children were admonished to stay outside and play or at least not to bother her with questions.

A day or two after Papa went by himself to Long View to preach Miss DeeLee's funeral, Grandma Esther came into Shiloh and helped Weegie and me to pack two bags with things to take to her house in the country. Mama was tired and nervous, she explained, and needed a lot of quiet, so we were going to stay with her until time for school to start.

Mama cried when we left. She had been crying most of the time, lately, bursting out suddenly at the table or when we were all in the living room, just sitting and reading or playing while Papa studied. Papa would look unhappy and helpless and tell her there was nothing she could have done, but she would only look at him as if she didn't believe him, and her face would take on that still, sad look of thoughtfulness.

Done about what? I gathered that all of the unsettling vibrations emanated from the circumstances of Miss DeeLee's death, but I could not understand why there should be so much unhappiness if Miss DeeLee had simply gotten her wish to go and join the people she loved best.

On Saturday Grandma Esther took me and Weegie to the little settlement that Long View folk called town. She delivered a carton of fresh eggs to Miss Stone, the telephone operator. We stood in the door of the tiny building and waited for her to count out change. She had to start over several times after stopping to plug in some more wires. She was beginning to shake her head and bring up the subject of "poor Miz Wills" when Grandma Esther said we had a lot of errands and pushed us ahead of her up the street.

She wanted to go in the Mercantile and have Miss Lottie cut her off some lengths of material from the new fall bolts. She agreed for us to stay outside and play on the sidewalk, warning us not to go far, for she would be back soon.

The morning had been chilly, and a skiff of early-fall mist was just rising and dispersing in ghost-like puffs. So the sun felt good as it shone warmly on the brick wall and on the cobblestones in front of it.

The hardware store was next to the Mercantile, and several loafers were already stationed at their daily positions in front of it. One young man in an old soldier's uniform was hunkered down with his arms resting on his knees and his hands locked in front of him. He seemed to be dozing. Several others were sitting on nail kegs lined up against the wall so that it served as a support for their backs. They would all talk at once and then get quiet for a while, clicking their teeth or chewing tobacco with liquid smacks. Already, fresh splashes were on the stones around them, looking like huge, flat brown bugs with many legs.

I was growing bored with staying in this one spot and was peeping into the door of the Mercantile to spy out Grandma Esther in the dimness at the rear of the long room, stretching some material from her nose to her arm's length to measure it. Weegie had made up a game of hopscotch and was playing it on the stones.

Just then a newcomer joined the loafers, and they all roused up enough to speak. It was a drummer coming out of the hardware store carrying a big black case in one hand and a Coca-Cola in the other. He had on a bright plaid suit and a new-looking felt hat with an orange feather. He talked loud.

"Whatcha say, boys?" He put down the big case and sat on it, then threw his head back to let half the drink go gurgling down his throat. I watched the ripples disappear under his collar, fascinated and a little bit repelled.

"Nothin' doin'," said one of the men.

"What's goin' on up the pike?" the younger loafer asked, proving that he was awake after all.

"Just the same old six and seven. You know." The drummer took another swig and looked off up the street as if he craved better entertainment.

The man on the keg next to him said, "I reckon we've had a purty newsy time around here lately. Don't guess you would have heard about it."

"Not that I know of. What was it?" I could tell that the drummer didn't expect much, and I didn't either. But I edged closer, for I wanted to hear whatever it was.

"Well, Old Lady Wills—you wouldn't know her—she just up and slit her throat from ear to ear, is all."

The drummer straightened up to listen. Weegie had heard that too, and both of us stood as if we had turned into statues, with our backs to the sidewalk and the men, listening in horror and disbelief.

"Let me take a guess. Man trouble mixed up in it," said the drummer.

"Lord, naw. Not Old Lady Wills. Naw, I don't know nothin' 'cept she musta went clean off her rocker. 'Course, she always *was* peculiar."

"I think you'd have to say," came from another keg, with spitting time taken out, "that she was just about the *most* peculiar person around."

"Did her old man find her?" asked the drummer, unwrapping some chewing gum and tossing the shiny paper right at our feet without noticing us.

"Aw, naw, he's dead of a stroke," answered the first old man, disgusted at the drummer's ignorance. "Naw, it was one of the men from over at the church come to check on her. Mr. Melton—you don't know him—"

"Ross."

"Aw, well. He don't know him. Anyways. He went around to the back yard when he found the house open and quiet. And there she was, all spread out on her back. You don't know how it is, but they's a little patch of white gravel around the back door, before the patches of grass start, and she was on that, in her church clothes—all dolled up and nowhere to go, as the feller says. Well, sir, the man 'at found her said he at first took it she had fell, and then he saw them spots on the gravel and two or three ignorant old domineckers peckin' away, thinkin', I reckon, that it was grains of red corn."

He paused to put a fresh cud inside his lips and then continued.

"The feller—Ross—leaned over her then and saw her insides, seemed like, spilling out, and the butcher knife glitterin' right there by her hand. They say old Ross with his Sunday-go-to-meetin' clothes on looked like a stuck hog hisself when he raised up from there."

I felt sick, and I wanted to run away, but I had to hear it all. Weegie's hand was cold as it tightly encircled my wrist.

"Old Beemer there might let you in on his little proposition," the soldier loafer told the drummer with a laugh.

"How's that?" asked the drummer, getting up and rubbing the small of his back as if preparing to move on.

"Well, I told all these fellers—and I allow I'm safe to include you: I'm ready to give a ham o'meat to the one that'll go all by hisself in the dark of night and just set a spell in the Wills' back yard. Alone and at night, mind you. I don't have a hankerin' to go myself, but anybody else is welcome."

Grandma Esther came out during the general laughter that followed this, and she must have heard Mr. Beemer's last speech, for she looked furious. She put the brown package tied with twine under her arm and, grabbing each of us by a hand, literally dragged us up the sidewalk.

I knew that Weegie was haunted by our discovery, too—for a while. Sometimes, during the winter, she had nightmares and awoke me with her crying. We never talked about it, not a word, but when we passed Miss DeeLee's house, we all looked in some other direction, each one groping with images already too vivid to need feeding by a new view.

By summer, though, we were able, to some degree, to move the experience we could not otherwise handle into the realm of play, somehow ridding the memory of part of its shocking quality by transmuting it into mock ritual.

That summer Junior and Sofey, black twins of an age between Weegie and me, came over almost every afternoon that we were with Grandma Esther, and we played and romped until dusk. Often someone (never I, to the best of my memory) would say, "Oh, let's play 'Miss DeeLee.'" Weegie always got to be "it" in this game, for I certainly didn't want to, and the twins, eager as they were to play , were scared to take the starring role. So Weegie would prolong the suspense for a few moments, and then she would scream, piercingly, flourish a stick across her neck, and reel backward upon the ground. Junior and Sofey were the terrified discoverers, bending over the "body" and moaning and hollering until, convinced by their own and Weegie's actions, they ran trembling to a far corner of the yard, the whites of their eyes shining, and there they would huddle in each other's arms until Weegie jumped up and ran over to them to break the spell.

The last time I participated in the game, even as a morbidly interested spectator, Weegie added a note of realism that brought the whole thing back to me in a way that was unbearable. Without warning, that time, she fell back on the bare ground by Grandma Esther's chicken house. Then, while the twins were screeching out, "Miss DeeLee, oh, Lawd!" her wrist moved, and a shower of red droplets fell around her in the brown dirt. Junior and Sofey yelped in surprise and terror and rolled over and over on the ground. Sickened, I recognized that Weegie had pulled the petals from one of the roses blooming over by the garden gate.

Throughout that summer and the next, when the Ross grandchildren or the twins were there, we dared each other to go breathtaking distances into the woods to catch lightning bugs. Someone would sneak upon one of the rest of us and shout, "Miss DeeLee!" and all of us would knock against each other and leap over fallen saplings in a mad rush to get back to the known and the safe.

Thus childhood passed, with subtle and mostly softening changes in me; and memories of the Willses gave way, at least on the surface of consciousness, to necessary grapplings with the crises implicit in the process of growing up. Papa, at last, stopped preaching at Long View except on the all-important Homecoming Day. After a time, Grandma Esther, who had been our second mother, was taken from us, and our visits to the farm became limited to occasional summer excursions or business trips to check on the activities of tenants.

Years later, Miss DeeLee was brought forcefully back to the top of my mind, and I realized that she had never been really far away. The truth was that the Miss DeeLee I thought I knew and the Miss DeeLee whose shocking deed had belied all my knowledge had been melded into myself so that what I was was never completely unrelated. She had remained with me to haunt me as a problem I had been unable to solve—and, somehow, as a duty I had left unattended.

I was in the midst of college activities, during my second year, when an attack of influenza confined me to my dormitory room for a week. As I lay there, impatient and bored but still too weak to get up and attempt anything constructive, I left off following every crack in the ceiling, worrying along the circuitous trailings, and began to read the names on the quilt that had been made for Mama when she became engaged. Names in flowery script or in painful little square letters were embroidered in contrasting colors on blocks of faded material, no doubt scraps from the very dresses that they wore to church or to parties. Most of the names I could not identify; a few I could guess by the first names, though they wore other last names by the time I knew them.

There, near a border, was a name I knew: written in black on dark pink material was "D. L. Wills." I tried to imagine how she had looked threading a needle and picking out her name for Mama's quilt.

"What an odd way to write her name—'D.L.'" I thought, almost idly.

But probably that reopening of my hoard of Miss DeeLee memories accounts for my visiting her grave for the very first time. I was home for Christmas holidays, and I decided to drive out to Long View to gather pecans for baking. Somehow, it seemed important that I make the trip alone before Weegie arrived home from Clarksdale Junior College.

When my burlap bag was full and lumpy, I decided to stop by the church building. As a child I had played among the stones many times, careful not to disturb flowers or step on the mounds. But I had never ventured to the corner where the Willses lay side by side; for by the time the stones were erected, the night-mare-pictures had been engraved too deeply into my mind.

I found Mr. Albert's grave straightway, but I was suddenly confused. The small marker for Percy Albert was there, with a mildewed angel perched at his feet. But the adjacent stone was surely not Miss DeeLee's. I went closer to read the words. The rest of it was all right—all but the name. It said, "Daisy Leona Davis Wills."

All of a sudden there flashed upon me a truth that con-founded me. I had not even known her *name*. How presumptu-ous I had been to assume that I knew *her*, to feel that she was, in a way, my private possession! All of those years when I had thought and puzzled, when I had so wanted to invade the very mind of her, behind that veil, I was perhaps no nearer than were any of the others. She had looked into my eyes, and I had seen *myself* reflected there, but I had not seen *her*. And, after all, was that the way it always was? Had to be?

It was a bitterness in me to accept that, whatever there was to see, know, understand, I had been as blind as the rest, only more prideful in my efforts to gain special entry. I hated that veil, but it was hers, and it was never removed!

As I touched the rough stone, I told myself, with a coldness that was like a final farewell, that now nothing could be done except to close a drawer and seal off an aroma that was more familiar to my secret self than my own body-scent. I stood lonely and alone, scarcely able to endure the foolishness of it all.

Exit Miss Tish

"Clifford, hon, just look at that picture frame, will you? Can't you see that hanging between our two front picture windows? Even the colors in that precious portrait would go just perfect with our living room suite."

Taking her husband's arm and steering him a few feet away from the casket to gain a better perspective, Mrs. Gaines turned to explain to the two or three other "mourners" who had been standing in small groups chatting quietly until Mrs. Gaines's voice captured their attention.

"I just *love* antiques," she explained, pointing to the painting which was placed on a tripod near the head of the closed coffin.

From the much admired frame a young Tish Ward looked at those who came and went on soft feet, as unmoved as they at the occasion which had brought them together at this place. Throughout the day those who wished to pay their respects moved toward the place where Miss Tish lay; the plush carpet prevented sounds of their approach. Subdued voices had consistently remarked on the beauty of the pall of red roses glowing almost vulgarly against gray metal. Then tribute was paid to the few floral arrangements tastefully placed nearby. With the briefest of glances upon the moveless countenance of the girl in the picture, they stepped back and, as if relieved, began to talk to each other about more comfortable, everyday topics. If, when they moved away from the area that reminded them of old mortality, their voices grew disrespectfully loud, there was no accusing response from Miss Tish or degree of change in the unruffled gaze which some artist had skillfully, and perhaps accurately, fixed there decades ago.

Nobody in attendance on this day, except for three tottering relatives whose memories were clouded, recalled that slim, self-contained girl who sat gracefully in front of a piano, turned on the bench so that her body curved softly—whether demurely or seductively an unacquainted observer would be left to wonder. Her left arm and long-fingered hand rested lightly on the keyboard. The artist had painstakingly depicted—in accordance with her firm command?—the sapphire ring which had been her mother's and which she wore constantly from the time her father bestowed it upon her to honor her eighteenth birthday. As her hands grew somewhat plump through the years, she transferred it to her little finger, where it must even now be trying in vain to send tiny darts of light into the gloom of the coffin. Atop the gleaming piano a vase of pink roses perfectly complemented the wide sash which circled young Tish's minute waist and made a splash of color against yards of gossamer white material comprising her gown.

Most of those who dropped by the Claymore Funeral Home to pay their respects during the hours prior to the scheduled memorial service could muster only vague images of Miss Tish at any age. Some of the younger men, who had come in from Shiloh on their lunch hour, recalled her tenure as their Sunday school teacher at the Shiloh Methodist Church, beside which raw new earth and a tent marked where she would be taken the next morning. It was their youthful recollections that they shared as they signed the guest register and then stood around for a few minutes with obvious dis-ease. One or two brought up pleasant memories of the famous Easter egg hunts that had been a Ward tradition kept alive by Miss Tish for many years. Some who had not grown up anywhere near Shiloh chimed in to say that they had heard of those hunts. Miss Tish and Willie Edwards, whom she counted on to do whatever was needed, would work for days getting the lawn as smooth as a piece of velvet and the shrubs perfectly clipped; then on the Saturday before the great day, they would break their backs bending to secrete hundreds of colored eggs for squealing hordes to discover and pile into little baskets which were lined up in readiness on the side porch. Somehow this cheerful snippet of life warmed the room and lifted a weight.

The only person in the room who felt that she *knew* the one they had come to honor was Ida Mae Brown, Miss Tish's neighbor and, as circumstances or fate had dictated, sole proprietor of all the facts about Miss Tish's final attack and her death. It was all she could do to listen to all the talk that went on in that funeral parlor without putting in her part. Easter egg hunt indeed! Who was it lived right up the road from the old Ward house where everything that went on was clear as day from her kitchen window or her front porch if she cared to look? Many a time she would lounge in the swing with her feet propped on a block of wood to keep them from swelling, and visitors would sit in the rockers while she made the old chains creak to accompany her tales of what all happened and didn't happen just across the field at the big house. She could lean forward and point around the vines that were trained on wires to keep out the evening sun, and they could look that way to see the tall white house with porches all the way around, and tiny fenced balconies protruding from upstairs windows.

She smiled and nodded when a young man stopped talking and seemed to expect her to respond. Well, she thought, smoothing her dress around her hips and looking around at the few who were there, she had had plenty of opportunities to share what she knew, and now that Miss Tish's story was over, there would be suitable occasions to pull it all together.

Here in the funeral parlor, of course, she knew what her part was: she had welcomed every single visitor all day long and told them little things they wanted to know. She made an effort to temper the force of her voice as well as to maintain a properly subdued countenance. And she tried to use good taste in choosing the comments she made about Miss Tish. Once she had decided what to share, the rest was easy: everything she said was a quotation from her own familiar text. She could stop or start anywhere and, after interruptions, go right back to her place and continue.

By inference and by facial expressions, she communicated quite clearly that there were *worlds* of stories about the poor dead lady which she, and she alone, could share at a proper time and place. She might not be as high-falutin' as Miss Tish had always set herself up to be, but she most certainly knew how to act.

A slight growl coming from her stomach reminded her that it was past noon and that the four relatives had probably had an early breakfast. Since only two or three were in the parlor, standing in a cluster away from the casket and talking in low tones, she decided it would be perfectly acceptable for her to check in the hospitality room. She whispered to the niece, Mrs. Letitia Yaeger, that she would go check on lunch.

Sure enough, one of the tables in the long room across the hall had "Ward" written on a small sign, and on it were piles of sandwiches, several salads, and four or five cakes and pies. Looking over the display and obviously preparing to leave were two women that she knew from Shiloh. They turned around when she spoke and explained that the coffee was made and lunch was ready. They were friendlier than usual, Ida Mae thought— probably because they were aware of the role she was being forced to play because there was nobody else to do it. She rejected the idea of taking them to meet the Ward relatives, though. After all, they were not the old lady's friends. They were on the Food Committee at Shiloh Methodist, and it was their month. But she didn't mind talking to them a while her-self. She owed them that much.

"Yes, there's no question that she's better off. Lord knows what she done with herself rattling around in that big old barn day in, day out," she said. She shuffled the salads to the front and moved the desserts toward the back.

"If she knowed what was good for her, she would have sold the whole kit 'n caboodle long ago and moved. Ed Bishop would have grabbed it in a minute for a pretty penny and turned it into a nice subdivision. She could have put her up a neat little modu-lar home near town, handy to everything. I know that's what I'd do. And whoever gets it probably will do it now."

The two ladies couldn't have agreed with her more. "'Course, it used to be that yard—*lawn*, 'scuse me—was just like Barton Park, all the time. Miss Tish was bound and determined to keep it the way it had always been, and as long as that Willie was around, to hop when she said, 'rabbit,' it worked out fine. Willie died, though, and you see when you pass by what a wooly mess she had to let it get in."

She read a question in their faces, and they weren't in that much of a hurry to leave. "Willie Edwards, I'm talking about. He was the Black feller used to work all the time for the Ward fam-ily. Mr. John counted on him to tend to things—oh, the cattle and the hay and everything else you could name. Then after Mr. John went and things was cut down about to nothing, most of the cattle hauled off to market, Willie wasn't needed, not all the time. But Miss Tish still used him for all sorts of things. Yes, Miss Tish thought she couldn't do without Willie. Sometimes I wanted to say, 'You got *me*, you old silly!' But anyway. After he went to work at the Ford plant, he'd still come by, after work or on Satur-days, to help out in the house or to do outdoors things."

Ida Mae could tell they were interested, a little bit, but she knew what to say when, so she thanked them for bringing the food and walked with them partway down the hall.

Not a soul was in the parlor except the four tired-looking relatives. They glanced toward Ida Mae, who bent toward them in case they had trouble hearing.

"I don't know if you all are used to this way of doing, but there's a lunch prepared for you in the Hospitality Room, we call it. I thought, while there's this little lag, you might like to have a bite, to get your strength up for the service. It'll probably be a mad house in here the last hour."

Before she had finished, Mrs. Yaeger and her son, Arthur, had already risen, and the two old men—John and Ward, she heard their sister call them—were doing their best to escape the soft depths of the sofa. They quickly followed her across the hall and with few instructions began to fill their plates. When they were seated at the round table, Arthur went back and poured each of them a cup of coffee. They didn't appear to notice the crowded table at the other end of the room, where another family from the other parlor had assembled and had already begun to eat and talk at the same time.

Ida Mae saw Arthur craning his long neck to scan the cabinet top, and she stepped over and brought back a bowl of sugar.

"Lovely food, Mrs. . . . . Brown," said Miss Tish's niece. "Did you prepare it yourself?"

Ida Mae laughed louder than she meant to. "Law, no, Betty Crocker and me are not very close friends. But what I was just thinking, your Aunt Tish would turn over in that fine coffin if she could see y'all eating out of paper dishes." The white of her teeth flashed whiter in contrast to the intriguing gaps as she laughed again, but in a more subdued manner. She believed she had the feel of these strangers enough that she could tell them some things about a relative she knew better than they did.

"They's all kinds of craziness in this world," she said musingly. "Lots and lots of times I'd go up there and she'd be eating her pitiful little dinner on that long wood table in the dining room—on her fancy china with real silverware and all. Like as not, if it wasn't a killing frost yet, she'd have a vase of flowers sitting there in front of her, just for nobody but hers truly."

They continued to reach across each other to replenish their plates, not talking to each other any more than to her. Since they didn't seem to mind her talking about Miss Tish, she drew up a chair to the end of the table and talked on.

"After the girls was married and moved out, I took to going up there now and then myself, just to help out a little, and it kind of growed. Sometimes she'd call me up and ask me to come over and help her with this or that. Aggravatin' thing was—if y'all will excuse me for saying so—when she asked, it was more like she was *tellin'*. Anyhow, I went because I knew she needed me. She's always been a right plump old soul, but I've never seen her show no more strength than a flea. I may be stove up in my feet and back, but at least I'm strong.

"If you knew her much, you're probably surprised she allowed a telephone in the house. I'll bet she never called up your mama to catch her up on things or wish her a 'Merry Christmas,' the way normal people do. Well, she wouldn't have had it except Mr. John had one put in, and 'course she wouldn't have it took out. It's so high on the kitchen wall, to fit *him*, I reckon, that she had to tiptoe to talk into it. And the way she hollered into the receiver would make you know she didn't half believe in tele-phone wires, anyhow. 'Course, she just used it for business. She wouldn't ring up anybody to palaver, even if it was right there in Shiloh. Like me, I don't know what I'd do to *rest* if I didn't have my phone next to my couch where I could stretch out and talk to my friends. What's life all about, anyway?"

They had gone through the sandwiches and salads with good appetites, and now they headed to the table for desserts, except for Mrs. Yeager. Arthur brought her a slab of banana cake with thick caramel icing. (I have to try that later, Ida Mae decided.) Then Arthur went back to the table and loaded his plate with a generous sample of each offering. It made Ida Mae wonder how he stayed like a skinny beanpole, the way he dug in.

"Another thing you won't believe," she continued while they ate and sipped coffee. "That old woman never did own a TV. Not even a black-and-white. What do you imagine she done with herself? It's no wonder if she got a little *off*."

"Did she keep up with her music?" Mrs. Yaeger asked. "Mama used to say that she had a real talent."

They were thinking of her in the portrait, Ida Mae imagined. "Lord, no, her little old hands were too bent and knotty with arthritis to plunk a tune on that piano. I don't know, maybe she just meandered from room to room picking up those old things of hers that makes me a nervous wreck when I dust, because I'm scared I'll break something. Antique lovers would probably be crazy enough to pay good money for them. Me, I'd a lot rather have something new, wouldn't y'all?"

They didn't answer yes or no, but she could tell they were listening and picturing things.

Ward Smith pushed aside his plate, with only a piece of pie crust left, and cleared his throat. Ida Mae was surprised at his high, quavery voice.

"Did my Aunt Tish never consider marriage?"

"'Course I never knew her in her young day. I *do* know that she had prospects at one time. 'Course, she wouldn't tell a person nothing, except what to do next. But once, I was in her big old bedroom trying to straighten things up a little, and she happened to be off in the kitchen piddlin' at something. So I noticed this real old chest at the foot of her bed, and I might have thought I could get some clean bedclothes out of it. Anyhow, I opened it, and it was just like the smell of some kind of flowers that come out of it and spread over the room. I could tell it had to been her hope chest; it was crammed with all sorts of napkins and doilies and pillow cases—even a friendship quilt with names embroidered in blocks that used to be white. I didn't have time to read any of them. They're probably all dead and gone anyhow."

She hated to disappoint her listeners by admitting that she didn't know what happened to stop her from marrying.

"But they say it was Mr. Philip Waite, you don't know him, but he's the one who owned all that land on the other side of the road from the Ward place. They say he called on her every Sunday of the world, for years and years, but nothing came of it in the end because Mr. John Ward made Miss Tish think *he* just couldn't do without her."

The relatives listened with interest, not seeming to question, any more than Ida Mae's audiences usually did, the trustworthiness of the mysterious "they" who, without any plausible source of intimate information, had accumulated and disseminated details of the plot of Miss Tish's fully developed private drama. It remained only for Ida Mae to supply structure and script, so to speak. Thanks to her enthusiastic and expert narration, there evolved a picture of Miss Tish with infinitely more capacity for tickling simple imaginations than glimpses of the real-life performer had ever possessed.

Ida Mae was gratified and a little relieved that these strangers—who had been strangers to Miss Tish too—willingly listened to her account without any sign of disbelief or skepticism. She took as a sign of their involvement the funny picture of Arthur with a daub of Fannie Tucker's meringue on the end of his long, skinny nose, and his mother did not even notice and tell him.

Most people were interested in Miss Tish's love life, if any. Ida Mae recounted how the young Tish, the girl in the picture, began to be courted by Philip Waite soon after she returned from a girls' finishing school in Boston—which nobody could believe Mr. John had given up for her to go to in the first place. Every Sunday of the world, Philip backed his car out of the barn where it sat all week and drove down the road and up the Wards' lane. Anybody who cared to look could mark off another Sunday, one thirty in the afternoon, just by watching him park up close to the side porch, slam the car door, straighten his good dark suit coat and bow tie, and march right up banistered steps to the front porch.

What happened inside the house during those long Sabbath afternoons was a matter for speculation. No witnesses could report. But "they" pictured them sitting side by side on the little sofa with its curved back and fancy carved wood along the edges. On the wall above them was the portrait of young Miss Tish at her piano, the same instrument sitting over near the heavily draped window. And there they would stay, with perhaps a period when they sipped tea and nibbled on little cakes which she brought to the parlor on a silver tray. When it was time to do the feeding and other chores, he would leave and drive away. Did she watch as he turned slowly into his lane and disappeared from sight?

"All that's a bunch of 'maginings," laughed Ida Mae. "So is the part about their spats over whether she would leave her papa and go with Philip. Well, she stayed.

"Then, one of them Sundays, at the end of the evening, he left like always, drove up to his lane and turned in, exactly like always. Next thing, he stopped and spilled over the steering wheel and died, just like that.

"See, that was long after Mr. John shriveled up and died, and still she hadn't changed anything. So when she went to the funeral, she sat off to the side, not with family. And she didn't faint, the way some expected her to. A lot of ladies used to. But she went home without showing anybody how she felt or saying a word."

"Now here's the peculiar part," she declared, leaning over and tapping the niece on the shoulder. "It seemed like Philip Waite left all that land and all that money—every living thing he had—to her. And them not married or anything."

Arthur and his mother leaned forward in surprise and interest, encouraging Ida Mae to go on. John was sound asleep, his chin resting on his chest, and Ward merely looked a question without moving in his chair.

"Not as much changed after that as you would expect. Mr. Waite's nephew and a big lawyer at that—it's Bob Taylor, you might have seen him come in with me this morning—well, he used to come by and check on her a lot. Anyway, we set in to wonder would she start spending in ways we could tell. 'Course, the Wards have always had plenty, but sometimes people like that are *poor rich*—you know what I mean?—no *loose* money to buy things and nicen up your house.

"Well, she built a new pasture fence—or had Willie to. That's about all I could tell. But if she got much out of Philip Waite's will, she sure didn't use it to better herself any. That would have been a perfect time to get a TV and a kitchen linoleum—and maybe some nice Venetian blinds like everybody else is getting. I would have. But everything stayed like it was, like it had been for 'bout a hundred years. I ought to know because I was up there two, three days a week to do little things she needed done. If there'd been any changes, I would have noticed."

Well, Ida Mae thought, rising from the chair and straightening her skirt over her hips, I've told them a good bit. I owe it to them. She needed to tell them about Willie, and then it would be time to get in place for the service.

"I believe I saw some friends from Shiloh step into the parlor. Excuse me a minute, I'll be back."

It was two ladies from up the road beyond Miss Tish's house. Ida Mae had never become personally acquainted with them, but she knew they had dropped in on Miss Tish a few times to see how she was doing.

"Thank you for coming," she said softly, directing them toward the casket. They both looked at the picture, which had slats of light and dark made by the sinking sun coming through the big end window.

One lady leaned over and touched a rose on the pall. "Lovely," she said, and Ida Mae and the other lady nodded.

They said they couldn't stay for the service, but they just had to pay their respects.

"I appreciate that," Ida Mae said. She turned back to the Hospitality Room as they went down the hall toward the front door.

She covered the congealed salads and found room for them in the refrigerator. Taking her time, she went over what she was going to tell them now. She always liked to build up to the part about Willie. They watched her as she went back and forth from the cabinet to the refrigerator and were clearly waiting for her to start talking. She sat back down where she had sat before, next to John, who was awake and ready to listen with the others. She could tell they had been doing some discussing while she was out of the room.

"See, one of the days I was supposed to go across to Miss Tish's house, I decided to wait for the mail to run. It was the day for the county paper, so I wasn't in too big a hurry. I would just rest my feet a while and glance over the local news. It was the first I knew about Willie's death. It was on the front page because there had been a bad wreck out toward the Ford plant, and a big tank truck had rammed into Willie's old truck and smashed his life out of him, just like that. Wham!

"Well, I couldn't wait to get myself over to Miss Tish's to see if maybe I'd be the first to let her know. I could imagine how she'd fall apart, for that Black man was the only one she depended on. I wanted to be there to support her if I could. Usually the back door was unfastened, but this time it was locked tight, and she wouldn't answer me, even after I knocked my knuckles raw and kept hollering out her name.

"She'd already heard, all right. I don't know if she went to the funeral. I asked her a few days later, when I went back to help her, but she ignored my question—she was always good at that, I tell *you*—and acted as if nothing had happened. Oh, 'scuse me, I'll be right back."

She had glimpsed an elderly lady hesitating in the door of the parlor. As she came up behind her, she could tell that she had never seen her before, but she immediately had the feeling that she was some kind of lady, the way she held herself and the closed, calm look she wore on her face as she turned to look at Ida Mae.

"I'm Mrs. Brown, a close friend of dear Miss Ward. Were you a childhood friend?"

"Oh, no, I did not know her then." She acted as if she wanted to keep looking at the portrait. Then she turned back to Ida Mae.

"I helped Miss Ward for years at Lovelady's Department Store. It was always a privilege to wait on her. She was truly a fastidious lady."

And I guess you are too, Ida Mae thought, noting the expensive-looking hat and shoes and purse, all soft and shiny and blue. Her dress was blue with long sleeves, and still she looked cool as a cucumber.

The undertaker was placing two rows of chairs behind the sofa where the family members would sit. She had assured him and Mr. Bob Taylor had too that not many would come to the service, since not many knew her anymore. Maybe a few would wait and drop in at the cemetery the next morning.

The lady obviously planned to stay for the service, so Ida Mae escorted her to a chair. She sat quietly with her feet flat on the floor and the purse in her lap under snow-white gloves. Somehow she looked like a mourner.

Ida Mae walked fast across the hall, for time was giving out. Arthur was finishing pouring coffee into his mother's cup. The two sipped while they looked straight at her.

"As time passed, though, the old lady started to act as if her thoughts had got tangled. I hate to say it, but I couldn't help noticing. We'd be taking care of whatever she'd dreamed up for us to do, and out of the blue she'd stop in her tracks and look at me—I mean, straight at me, like she never used to do—and ask, 'Did I tell you that Willie was dead?' I'd still be thinking that over when maybe in just a few minutes she'd go over the same thing: 'Did I tell you that Willie was dead?'"

Ida Mae had to shake her head at all this. "You can imagine how funny that made me feel! I started to wonder, just for about a minute, if *I* was the crazy one. I never have known how to take people who're not *right*."

The niece, Lettie as they called her, looked a little upset to think of her relative losing her mind. "Ward, John, did you ever know of that kind of weakness in the Ward family?" They shook their heads vigorously.

"Was she . . . like that to the end?" Arthur inquired as if he might make a scientific study.

"To the very end," Ida Mae assured him. And the end was what she remembered most clearly. She had told the ambulance driver that night when Miss Tish was in the back maybe dead that she would never forget a detail. And she had told it to several people since then. She still couldn't believe it had been her who was on the scene when Miss Tish was hit by whatever it was that killed her.

She told them how it had come to be. She had gone over to the big house in the early afternoon because Miss Tish had mentioned wanting her feather bed to be sunned and aired. So as soon as she arrived, she went on back to the big bedroom and dragged the feather bed down the hall and out onto the side porch.

"I was beatin' the fire out of that old feather bed with a broom handle and trying to hold my head on one side so I wouldn't choke to death. I 'bout wrenched my bad back, but I didn't even notice it till I climbed up in that ambulance and we started toward town with the sireen screaming. Anyway. Something told me to quit and step over to where I could see in the kitchen. My land, what a sight! I'm glad you all never had to see your aunt looking like that."

"What was it?" The niece asked aloud, but the others were leaning toward her. She stood up to be able to tell it better.

"Well, Miss Tish was standing there by the doorjamb, like somebody had pushed her into the corner made by the built-in cabinet. I'll show you how it was when you're at the house. She was staring into space with nothing moving in her whole entire face. The corners of her eyes were leaking a little, but it wasn't like real tears, and she didn't look sad—just *empty*."

Ida Mae had to use her hands and arms some to show how she worked to get Miss Tish eased into a kitchen chair and propped so she wouldn't slide right out onto the floor. She herself was dripping wet with perspiration from wrestling with Miss Tish's useless body, but shaking as if a chill had hit her. She offered the old woman a drink of water, but she jerked her head just enough to make the water spill out and wet her dress all the way down the front.

Ida Mae stopped, gave all that a moment to sink it, and then asked, as dramatically as she could, "And do you know what she kept saying all the time I hovered over her there, just hoping to get one ounce of sense out of her?"

When they didn't venture an answer to what was obviously a rhetorical question, she went on, "It wasn't very plain, it was like she'd been to the dentist and her face hadn't come to yet, but I understood it all right. Lord knows I'd heard it enough times. She kept muttering that same old crazy thing—'Did I tell you that Willie was dead?'"

"Right then," she concluded, "I knew she was goner. For one thing, she put me in mind of my Ab, who's been gone nine years come next month. So I propped her up the best I could and quick as a flash called 911. I hadn't hardly had time to drag that old feather bed back into the hall, in case it rained and in case she *did* fool me and get over this spell, when I heard the sireen bleating around the big curve up the road. We'll never know when the old soul would've been found if I hadn't been there."

Well, that was enough for now. There would be plenty of time to tell them worlds more up at the house. She had a feeling she knew who would be cleaning and sorting and trying to get stuff in order. But hadn't she always been willing to do all she was able to do?

Mrs. Yaeger glanced at her watch, and they all rose simultaneously, John with the help of Ward. They went in a little drove down the hall to the restrooms, and Ida Mae told them she would see them in a few minutes in the parlor. She put a few more things into the refrigerator and gathered up their paper dishes and threw them in the trash can.

I've got to have a few minutes to myself to pull myself together, she told herself. A person can take only so much in two solid days. Well, a night and a day, but she was tuckered out.

She made her way down the hall toward the restroom. She met the relatives as they joined after coming from the doors opposite each other. They went into the parlor. Let them sit there for a while like four birds on a clothes line, she thought. I can't be with them every minute, my lands.

Two ladies who worked in the Shiloh First National were leaning toward the mirror, applying new lipstick and palming their hairdos into place. They spoke to her reflection.

"We've been visiting in Parlor Two," one of them explained. "You're with Miss Ward, aren't you?"

She answered from a stall. "Yes, ma'am, and I've got to get back to there. But a person can only do so much, and your strength gives out. 'Course, I've had to take care of the relatives too. They don't know how we do things down here."

"Will they be living down here?" the other woman turned to ask as she placed herself before the mirror.

"Lands, no, they have never spent any time here, and they wouldn't fit in. No, I feel sure they'll be getting ready to sell. It wouldn't surprise me to look out of my kitchen window one day and see a bunch of bulldozers piling red dirt everywhere."

"Miss Ward was a private person, wasn't she?" one of them said.

"I reckon she was. And peculiar. I always say they's so many ways to be crazy." She reached down the collar of her mauve dress and tried to adjust her slip straps. "I don't want it to be snowing in the South when I march in there before all those people," she laughed. But that reminded her of something.

"I just wish you ladies could have seen her underclothes—Miss Tish's. Finest material you ever laid eyes on—and she washed it out by hand in Ivory. I saw her hanging it in the bathroom, is how I happen to know. Now, who else was ever going to lay eyes on them things to 'preciate, pray tell?" Again she laughed and slapped her thighs at the foolishness old, well-off people can sink into.

The minute the ladies said goodbye and left, she almost fell onto the bright-flowered love seat and threw her feet up on the low coffee table strewn with *Family Circle* magazines.

She peered under the stalls to be sure no feet were there. "Who would have dreamed I would have had this chance to do all I've done! And more comin'." She spoke aloud, to make it more real.

"If I didn't put my feet up a minute, the way I do at home, my feet and ankles would be swole in a strut," she said, checking them out from where her head was leaning against the back of the sofa. After all, she had to admit, she felt *good*. A person can do what she's called on to do.

When she straightened her hair and dress and went back to the parlor, two or three people were in the chairs. The clerk from Lovelady's sat with her back straight and her eyes still on the portrait. The niece had taken a chair at the other end of the sofa. It was hard for her to get out of the deep cushions.

Ida Mae spoke to the Reverend Walker and to Lawyer Taylor, who were over by the window discussing final arrangements.

It was nearly time to start. A candle stood at each end of the casket, making a little glow and picking up highlights in the red roses.

A late visitor peered into the parlor and then entered. Ida Mae rushed over to make her welcome. They talked low because nobody else was talking.

"Yes, ma'am," Ida Mae responded to a query. "I've been well acquainted with Tish for many years." She met the eyes of the lady with a look of pride and dignity. "And I'm the one who called 911!"

The Passing Night

"So this is what being 'bone-tired' feels like," Jason Wentworth thought, wearily letting the sleeves of his luxurious new jacket slip from his arms. He took it to the large cedar-scented closet and hung it beside the dress suit in which he would be married in less than twenty-four hours.

The cut and the softness of the jacket were a wonder to Jason's eyes and touch. He had never worn anything vaguely resembling it. But Merilee had said, when eagerly presenting it to him this evening, after their return from the Moores' party honoring them, that it would be absolutely perfect for the honeymoon and for later, when they were living back here together. She exclaimed over how nice he looked in it while he self-consciously stood before her for inspection.

"And it picks up the blue of your eyes *so* well," she said, looking at him with such warmth and admiration that he felt himself responding enthusiastically, to her and therefore to her gift. He expressed sincere gratitude, declaring that he would wear it until bedtime.

Of course, since he had never smoked, it would not have occurred to Martha, in all the thirty years they were married, to buy him a smoking jacket. At Christmas or on birthdays she gave him what she knew he needed and would be utterly incapable of buying for himself—underwear, socks, pajamas, handkerchiefs. And at other times, for no particular occasion, she would bring home a special book that had come into the store where she worked and leave it on his bedside table as a surprise. Often he would pull on the bulky shapeless sweater that seemed immortal because, when she deemed a particular model hopeless, she replaced it with another exactly like it. His hand would reach into a well-stretched pocket to discover a small volume of poetry, one of the Romantics or a new edition of sonnets—another treasure for the two of them to enjoy together.

Somehow, on this, the eve of his marriage to Merilee, he had been thinking of Martha all day, from the moment he awoke and faced the realities before him. At the party he kept imagining her responses and commentaries. He even pictured her smile—tolerant but definitely amused—when Merilee was helping him into the smoking jacket, and he half expected her to laugh aloud at Merilee's lavish praise of his "sky-blue" eyes and of his "darling figure" in the jacket. Martha's approval had always been *controlled* and, at its most cherished, tacit. When she did voice praise or communicate it with a look, he hoarded it in his heart and drew on it for needed strength.

On the other hand, her disapproval never smarted for long, for she never saw a foolish action as a cause to condemn *him*: she attributed such to a lesser part of him which it was her duty, as loving wife, to help him to thwart. He counted on her to ride to his rescue in the manner of a female version of Spenser's Prince Arthur—a symbol of "Magnificence," possessor of all virtues and therefore able to compensate for whatever lack might be found in him.

Moving back and forth in the room that was as strange as a hotel room in a far-off city, he thought ruefully of Martha's coming to his rescue, over and over. He stood by the sink with his hand hovering above the shaving supplies he was laying out in readiness for the morning.

Throughout the nearly thirty-one years of their union, there had been a string of young female admirers whose response to Jason was taken by him to be unmixed devotion to literature. After-class sessions in a quiet corner of the student center would grow into hours, with Jason oblivious to time as they pored over the text of some poem which the girl had earnestly begged him to explain. He would often quote long passages without referring to the book lying open on the table between them. His listener would sit mesmerized, her warm dark eyes glistening with—as they perhaps both thought—appreciation and understanding. He fed upon this contact of three souls—theirs and the spirit of the creator of the immortal work.

Jason smiled to remember Martha's sensible reaction. Time and again she would remark, not to nag, but to put the troublesome situation before them to be handled, "You're a fool for soulful brown eyes, Jason Wentworth." And he would see what must be done to set things right.

Not that he ever lost the joy of sharing his great love with minds hungering for enlightenment. But always there was no doubt that Martha was his true soul mate, the completion of himself. He would burst into the kitchen full of excitement about a session with a current protégé. Martha would be scurrying about putting together their evening meal, or she would be sitting at the little kitchen table waiting for loaves of bread to finish baking. She would place a finger on the passage she was reading, and she would listen, with the slightest of a smile, while his enthusiasm flamed anew at his reiteration of the topic.

Since her death, Jason had thought of this scene, of Martha in the kitchen, surrounded by the aroma of baking bread, as the one scene which most accurately encapsulated the meaning and worth of their life together. In his memory the warm, yeasty smell was laced with the excitement of shared thoughts and feelings with the intelligent woman who listened, sometimes disagreeing, sometimes offering an alternative interpretation. Then at last she would push her book out of the way of dripping butter while they each ate a piece of the first steaming loaf to be pulled from the oven.

In the two years since Martha's fatal and completely unexpected heart attack, Jason had groped for meaning and direction. He occasionally spent a few hours with the families of his son and his daughter, and he came away saddened by the worried looks he intercepted. They were helpless to supply his needs, and he sought no social contacts. Those had been Martha's doings.

The truth was that Jason was *afraid*. He had never been adept at handling relationships, and he knew that about himself just as surely as he knew that he possessed special insights and sensitivities which were both gifts and liabilities. Martha had known him best of all, and she had held firmly to reins which had allowed him to experience, at the same time, titillation and security. Since Martha was gone, he shied from dangerous or potentially threatening situations, knowing his limitations and sensing overwhelmingly his vulnerability.

The moment he saw Merilee Hopkins, all thought of caution fled his mind. It was last Christmas, and he had driven up from Clarksdale to spend a day or two with his old friends, the Moores, the oldest citizens in the oldest, most aristocratic section of Shiloh. They were holding an Open House, and they wanted Jason to be their house guest. He had been a roommate of their son Steve, who died many years ago, when he was in his twenties. Through the years Jason had kept in touch, visiting them whenever he could, rambling through their far-stretching fields and woods in all seasons. This was his first visit, though, since Martha's passing, and they all made strenuous efforts to push aside unvoiced thoughts of sadness and lose themselves in the seasonal festivities.

Mr. and Mrs. Moore, still energetic and bright-eyed though well into their eighties, were sitting side-by-side on a sofa in the much decorated parlor, all atwitter as they awaited the arrival of their guests. Jason was standing by the fireplace, savoring warmth on the backs of his knees. He was the first to see Merilee, coming from the direction of the back hall, looking everywhere and exclaiming over the holiday glory.

The Moores lifted themselves from the sofa and greeted Merilee with affectionate hugs. Mrs. Moore then took her by the hand and led her toward Jason, who hastened to meet them halfway.

"Jason, my dear, we've told you all about our sweet neighbor girl. Well, this is Merilee. Is she as pretty as we said?" She laughed, reveling in the license of old age.

Merilee took Jason's extended hand between her soft ones and looked beamingly into his face with the most beautiful, *speaking* brown eyes he had ever beheld.

"I've met the professor," Merilee declared. ("I could never have forgotten such a 'phantom of delight,'" Jason thought, aghast that his mouth was so dry he might not be able to speak.)

"Yes, I did—I heard you down at the Clarksdale Literary Club speaking about some poet. You were *wonderful!*" She squeezed his hand, and Jason felt electricity tingle to his elbow. Five minutes after they had met, under the delighted scrutiny of the Moores, his fate was sealed: he was certain that his long quest for the Ideal was at an end.

For Jason the evening proceeded in a haze of dizzying sensations. Individuals separated themselves from the buzzing crowd and made gracious overtures to him; he responded with appropriate good nature. But his eyes and his pulses waited upon another and yet another sight of Merilee. She moved with perfection of grace, unpretentiously assisting her elderly neighbor in performing the duties of hostess. She was obviously well acquainted with most of the guests and easily contributed to everyone's comfort and pleasure.

Jason tried to be subtle as he watched her every movement and greedily tried to glean her words from conversations she engaged in with various guests. When she left the room and shortly re-entered with a pitcher of punch to refurbish the gleaming silver bowl, he openly gaped in spite of himself. The arch of her lifted arm, pure marble in glowing candlelight, was art and music and poetry wedded into one breath-taking creation.

She turned to move away, and the sinuous swish and flow of her silver-pink dress sang to him a fairy song, awakening feelings he had not experienced in years. Upon the very image of her perfect form were superimposed in his head the lines of "Upon Julia's Clothes." Part of him wondered at himself, and part was wild to whisper those suggestive lines in her ear and call her "Julia," then watch to see a spreading blush do its best to improve upon perfection.

In a word, he was lost from the start, for there hovered in no corner of his being the wish to be saved. Indeed, to succumb to her charms was, he thought, to find himself, at last, by losing himself in the Ideal.

"Perfect soul in perfect body," he told himself and wondered that Fate had made him of all men most fortunate.

As Jason mused on the past months since he met Merilee, he realized that his work at the university had become the dream, his deepening involvement with Merilee his only reality. When he was in the classroom, the words and meter under scrutiny caught him up in their familiar magical spell, and the sentiments he labored to share with neophyte readers had never been more intensely relevant to his own needs. Sometimes, though, he sensed that the students *knew* of the fatal shift in the center of his being; and some days, when the class had ended, it seemed to him that there was a remoteness and unwonted coldness in their response to him—almost as if they were experiencing disillusionment, or even betrayal. Still it was Merilee who was his bread and drink and very breath. The winter somehow wore itself out and went.

They had long conversations on the telephone. He could hear her deep intakes of breath as she listened to quotations

spontaneously coming to his mind as perfect expressions of out-
looks and ideals which they shared.

On weekends he usually drove up to Shiloh, and they took
long drives if the weather was good; at other times they sat before
a fire in her parlor and talked for hours on end of the years that
they had lived before the miraculous converging of their paths.

He had known a great deal about her from the Moores' comments through the years. Yet, at first, when she freely spoke to
him of her prior marriages, he was aware of an irrational sense of
loss. The *fact* of her having been married a number of times—
three, he now learned—was no surprise to him. He recalled Mrs.
Moore's giving him more than once a fully detailed sketch of
"poor little Mary Lee" and her unfortunate experiences, through
which, however, she had come "with flying colors." Now, though,
when Merilee casually brought to life each of these major participants in her life history, providing names and details, he was
jealous, not of a body with which others had enjoyed the privi-
leges of intimacy, but of a mind and a soul which for a time had
focused totally on each of them.

Soon Jason had been able to rise above what from the start he
despised as littleness in himself; and he came to realize that everyone who had been a part of Merilee's existence was indeed his
benefactor. The compassion and understanding, the strength and
the warmth—though, no doubt, native traits—were developed to
this superior degree through a history of giving and suffering. He
became able to think of the three familiarly, with no sense of envy.

Still, on that night before the wedding, he was too weary to
control the flow of his mind; and just as surely as Martha hovered near in his thoughts, so were the personages of those three
husbands in the room—a room where at least two of them had
been. He washed his face and rubbed it hard with a luxuriant
towel, as if to exorcise unwelcome wraiths.

Merilee had first married an older man of the community,
a friend of her father almost his equal in age. For two years

following high school she had attended a girls' school in Virginia, in spite of her reluctance to leave her widowed father alone. Shortly after returning home, she agreed to marry Mr. Tucker—she always referred to him in this formal term—and lived with him on the other side of Shiloh, toward St. Elmo, for just over two years, nursing him through the fatal illness which made itself evident soon after they were married.

She was still involved in the complicated process of selling Mr. Tucker's house and land and settling his rather large estate when her father died, leaving her alone in the sprawling house in which she had grown up.

"For a while I didn't know which way to go," Merilee had said to Jason, touching his hand when she saw that his eyes were glistening with tears for the bereft young girl that she had been.

Then Lester LaFayette had come to Shiloh, as different from local settlers as was his name. He was a surveyor hired by the electric company to lay out rights-of-way for high-power lines, and their courtship was given added spice by the realization that circumstances would soon take him away.

"He didn't have any family around here, and he had a—I don't know, a *freedom*— about him. He made me laugh."

But the end of the story was scarcely humorous. Merilee and Lester worked up a hasty wedding, held in Merilee's own flower garden, with only a few in attendance, including the Moores and a dozen or so from the Methodist Church. They were ready straightway to take their leave. Lester had sold his car, and she had locked hers in the garage and given her house keys to the Moores, who sadly promised to watch after things.

She had felt that she was a bride for the first time, Merilee said, as she and Lester watched their piles of luggage being put on the twelve o'clock train. Then he helped her to climb onto the train to begin the trip to Chicago.

He had described his suburban estate to Merilee in such detail that she could easily picture its quiet luxury. "All it needs is the touch of a real lady," he had said the day of his proposal. Her acceptance had been quick.

For a few hours the newness of the train trip and of their altered relationship provided exciting distractions. Then, for reasons Merilee had not fathomed, even to the present day, Lester turned toward her on the leather train seat and began to tell her facts very different from anything he had told her before. His estate was, in fact, a complete work of fiction: he had very little to which to take a bride. But he still professed his love, vowing that his passion was the reason for his "doctoring the story up a little." "You and I, we'll make it together," he promised, in a tone which suggested that he had just finished sharing a pleasant anecdote.

Merilee had exited the train at the next station and somehow managed to retrieve her luggage. After spending the night in a rooming house on the square, in sight of the station, she had caught a morning train back to Shiloh.

Through the years the Moores had talked at great lengths about this part of Merilee's life. Even though he had never met her, this segment of her story drew sympathy from him. Mrs. Moore cried a little with every telling. "It still breaks my heart to think of that brave little soul holding her head high when you knew she was just *destroyed!*"

By the time she renewed a relationship with Elliot Larkins and married him, Merilee had become the most colorful ornament in the limited society of little Shiloh. She became involved in civic and social affairs in Clarksdale and even took two trips to Europe.

Life with Elliot seemed to be what she had always wanted. More trips to Europe, winters in his condominium in Florida, shopping sprees in New York—Merilee was happy at last! Then he died of a heart attack, and she was left to her own devices again. For five years she spent little time in Shiloh; there was not much there to meet her needs. When Jason met her, she was known to be a world traveler and an avid shopper and a wonderful conversationalist.

Jason could not surmise, from Merilee's autobiographical narratives, her exact or even approximate age. Age had never been a matter on which Jason had dwelled; it was a triviality that was irrelevant to *ideas*, which were timeless. Furthermore, figures of every kind had been left to Martha; they were, Jason willingly admitted, her forte. But the sequence of events would have to make Merilee about his own age, or a little older— the Moores had, in fact, indicated as much. Yet, when he was in her presence, the concept of *age* was utterly incompatible with the vision which invaded and overthrew his mind. Always perfectly attired and meticulously coiffured, she presented an image of timeless perfection. One did not think of cosmetics, so expertly were they applied; certainly Jason didn't. But even he had to assume that much expense and time went into the creation and maintenance of such flawless beauty. The luxury of having more than enough of both made possible her access to imitations of nature too subtle to be recognized as imitations at all.

The fragrance she wore haunted him in the hours when they were apart. Sometimes it clung to the fabric of his own sleeves and filled him with delight and loneliness. It was an indefinable aroma which, far from assailing the senses, bewitched them and lured him to unwonted paths where sweet flowers grew. She was his "belle dame," but she possessed all the "merci" of which even he, idealist that he was, had ever dreamed.

So complete was the spell which she worked over his entire being that he was wrenched from all native tendencies to be still and nurture a safe, bubble-enclosed euphoria. Endymion-like, he had glimpsed Ideal Beauty, and he must have it for his own. He was moved by a determination to take an action which would forever change the course of his existence. Without consideration of practical ramifications, he must take her to be his wife.

The time which chose itself was a late dinner following a community concert. She had arranged to spend the night with an old friend in Clarksdale so that they could enjoy a leisurely meal before having to part.

Christians' was the most elegant restaurant in Clarksdale. Its ambiance reminded Merilee of favorite establishments in New York—but even more, she declared on this occasion, of a fine old hotel dining room in London that she would so *love* to take him to.

Before he knew it, with the strains of Mendelssohn still tingling through his head and elbows, while they sat surrounded by velvet and candlelight and the delicate essence of violets, he heard himself asking her to marry him. He saw rather than felt his hands clinch into fists on the crisp blue cloth, and a part of his mind grasped the irony of the picture of him, Professor Jason Wentworth, cowering before the likelihood of rejection, dreading the disappointment of seeing their relationship spoiled by his own rashness.

What he saw next was a miracle of snow and pink rosebuds as her hands descended upon his and melted them with their warmth. Looking up at last into the depths of her peerless brown eyes, he read, not shock or even surprise, but serene acceptance. The excited play of words soon displaced awkward silence, and plans were being made that only weeks before would never have entered his mind even as vague possibilities.

She amazed him with the swiftness with which she was able to grasp their new situation and begin to formulate strategies, while his own mind was still backed off in shock. They could arrange everything in time to be married at the end of Spring Term, she assured him. They could have a simple ceremony in Shiloh and then take a brief trip—Jekyll Island would be nice, she thought; he would enjoy the scenery, and she always loved get-togethers with some of the regulars.

Jason leaned toward her across the table, captivated by the chant-like tone of her beautiful voice and moved by the natural manner in which, already, she joined the two of them by shaping "we" into a special syllable often repeated in her narrative.

"Then you can teach part-time this summer and a class or two in the fall, since you want to gradually cut down on your work. You can arrange to be off in the spring, and we can take a nice long trip to Europe. Of course, we'll have to work in the theater tour to New York in the fall. You will want to browse around some museums and libraries while I get in some good shopping for both of us. I know all the right places."

Jason was quiet for a few moments. He didn't recall ever intimating that he would consider relinquishing any of his classes: a life without the challenge of standing before new, fresh groups, facing malleable minds that could be challenged and won to an appreciation of immortal poetry, was one that he could not conceive. But soon he saw that Merilee was right, and he adopted her enthusiasm, looking forward to introducing her to choice literary havens that she had missed on all her earlier trips abroad. They would walk together through the shadowed streets of old Florence, where, as a young graduate student, he had spent a whole month communing with spirits who had created the beauties which were the chief dwellers of his mind. Merilee had been on a tour that stopped off for a day or two in Florence, she was almost sure. "But I know I didn't go to any cemetery. I always like to concentrate on the living, don't you?" She laughed and continued to flesh out their itinerary.

The remainder of winter and early spring passed like dreams in disconnected segments that, in Jason's waking hours, somehow seemed less palpable than those of his night visions. His colleagues congratulated him and then for the most part ignored his imminent change of life. Occasionally he intercepted a look that he could not exactly interpret—whether wonder or envy or pity he could not say. Merilee proclaimed a dinner at the Faculty Club a great success, declaring that it pleased her to be joining the ranks of "faculty wives," albeit for a short time.

There were several fetes in Shiloh, where Merilee's family was one of the oldest and most respected. Between what seemed endless social activities, Jason listened to Merilee's endless plans and couldn't help feeling somewhat overwhelmed.

"That Merilee can handle things," Mr. Moore often said with obvious admiration.

"Well, she's had to learn the hard way, the Lord knows," Mrs. Moore would respond, as if in defense. "Merilee can take care of herself the best of anybody I know."

The *public* Merilee more and more became an object of Jason's awe, but he yearned, with an actual physical ache, for the years when they could be alone to share quiet, private hours. He longingly pictured intimate evenings in front of his fireplace—or hers, Merilee having decided that their main headquarters would be her house, with Myrtle and Jasper already permanently installed there to help out. But he dreamed of the two of them warming to lengthy discussions that would lead them to go for book after book until they would end the discussion sitting together in the flickering firelight, with opened books strewn all about them in gorgeous disarray.

By the Saturday which was the eve of the long-awaited wedding day, Jason was aware only of a heaviness and a great desire for the preparations and the ceremony to be over. Merilee, in contrast, had seemed to relish every aspect of their courtship period, particularly since the wedding plans were announced. She blossomed before the eyes of all.

The Moores had arranged an early dinner party for Saturday evening, and, following his packing and a thought-filled drive up from Clarksdale, Jason had only enough time to put his dark suit for the wedding in Merilee's guest room closet and freshen up before it was time to leave in order to arrive ahead of the first guests.

Merilee's pale green dress enhanced her coloring to perfection. Jason's heart stirred with happiness that gripped like pain as they sat close together in the back of his car, the deliciousness of her scent enfolding him. Jasper drove them the short distance to the Moores' and, leaving them at the big side door, proceeded to town to have the car serviced and made ready for the trip to Jekyll Island.

The evening was one of easy cheer, full of laughter and congratulatory wishes. Jason succumbed to the mesmerizing aura filling the old-fashioned rooms, watching for every opportunity to capture Merilee's glance and extract strength from it.

He was relieved when everyone left and he and Merilee were free to say their goodbyes to the Moores, reiterating plans to meet them on the following morning at the nearby Methodist Church where they would attend services and then, immediately afterward, gather in the small chapel for the ceremony. Besides Jason's small family and his department chairman and his wife, only the Moores would be in attendance. The ceremony would be simple and brief, but elegant, Merilee had said from the beginning.

The Moores stood side by side on the edge of their big front porch and waved to them as they walked across the front yard to take the winding path through a strip of woods that gave way to an open field reaching to the edge of Merilee's lawn. The old couple were as happy as children to see two of their favorite people joining their lives. And to have Jason so near them—at least for much of the time—would be "almost like having our own dear boy back."

The usual night chill was hardly discernable; and, though the face of the moon ("Queen Moon," Jason said) was muffled by clouds, Merilee didn't need to take the tiny flashlight from her handbag until they were well into the woods. The circle of yellow she played along the path was not much larger than a firefly's puny efforts, but she held to his arm with her free hand, and they shuffled through a leaf-strewn path which they could not see. Night sounds surrounded them, in the bushes and in the branches above their heads. Jason began to recite one of his favorite poems, inspired by the setting. He began "Ode to a Nightingale" at its beginning and never faltered—though, as always, the emotion caught him up to supersaturate his being.

Forlorn! The very word is like a bell
    To toll me back from thee to my sole self!
Adieu! The fancy cannot cheat so well
    As she is fam'd to do, deceiving elf.
Adieu! Adieu! Thy plaintive anthem fades
    Past the near meadows, over the still stream,
    Up the hill-side; and now 'tis buried deep
    In the next valley-glades:
Was it a vision, or a waking dream?
    Fled is that music:—Do I wake or sleep?

His voice had become hoarse as he concluded. She squeezed his arm. "I declare, my professor could read a telephone book and make it sound special! That was a little sad, though—but pretty."

He felt a blanket of sadness cover him, for the fading images that his voice had created in the gray darkness. The enticing aroma of invisible flowers rose to his nostrils and over-powered the now-familiar subtle fragrance of Merilee.

She tightened her hold on his arm and spoke in a tone that drew him out of his contemplative mood.

"Would you listen to that? We're going to have a mighty early frost this year!"

She explained, when he asked her meaning, that the katy-dids, raucously arguing among the black branches, were the first she had heard this year, and that meant the first killing frost could be expected in exactly three months. She laughed to show that she didn't take the folklore seriously.

"But of course, *we* don't care, do we? We'll just go where the sunshine is. So there, you katydids!"

She was still laughing, the little laugh with separate syl-lables that blended into music, when they stepped out of the woods and into pale moonlight. It was easy to see the rest of the way to Merilee's house, which was just across the field and all lit up.

It was a lovely late-spring evening, but spangles of lightning were streaking the west with increasing frequency, and Jason heard a round roar of thunder as they entered the house.

Jason found it difficult to relax as they sat in the back parlor savoring the uniqueness of this, the last night which they would spend apart. The elegant smoking jacket, still smelling of an expensive shop, seemed to hug him too tightly, actually to constrict his shoulders and arms. It was Merilee, though, who suggested that they retire early because, she said, "There are miles between here and where we'll be laying our heads tomorrow night." She looked meaningfully into his eyes with a new degree of intimacy, and he felt a weakness in his knees as he arose to go upstairs.

They embraced at the foot of the spiral staircase. He felt the softness of her cheek pressed to his, perfectly smooth and only slightly moist.

"Now, remember, Myrtle and Jasper will be just down the hall if you need anything. Aren't we the circumspect pair, though, with *two* chaperones?" She had worked to convince him of the appropriateness of his staying in her home, explaining how it was the only practical arrangement under the circumstances—and perfectly proper besides.

Jason was so weary that his limbs were like alien weights that he was forced to hoist with great effort from step to step. He was glad to shed the heavy clothing that was further weighing his body down; he relaxed somewhat under the sharp, warm prickles of water as he showered.

He began to feel the return of familiarity with himself when he had pulled on his pajamas, crisp cotton, gray with maroon stripes, the exact kind that Martha always kept in good supply in his dresser drawer, and that the boys still gave him at Christmas. The blue silk ones that Merilee had bought him for the honeymoon trip were in one of his suitcases left in the trunk of the car.

He sat on the edge of the bed and succumbed to a strange urge to repeat to himself, alone in this room which he had never seen until today, the stanzas he had recited in the dark woods. When he had finished, he noticed that rain had begun to fall. Lightning flashed around the edges of the heavy draperies, and hard rain pounded on a tin awning over the window. He began to feel comforted and warmed, as though kindred spirits dried themselves in the room with him.

A gentle tap on his door surprised him. He tugged his robe about him and went, barefoot, to open the door.

"I thought about that old tin awning outside your window, and I was afraid the rain would keep you from your rest. We can move you to the other side of the hall if you like." He felt grateful for Merilee's unfailing concern.

She was sylph-like and shining as she stood in the doorway, a dazzling white robe drawn about her and tied at the waist with a wide gold belt. She was as beautiful as ever, but a something-different worried the corner of his consciousness.

As if she had observed his puzzlement, she put a hand to each of her cheeks and laughed, almost self-consciously. "This is Merilee without makeup, you might as well know."

But there was something else different—something more basic, which he could not at first identify. Then, as she looked at him with her customary concern and affection, it came to him: it was her eyes that were different! Unquestionably striking as they still were, they were no longer *brown*. Rather, they were a greenish gray, and he suddenly had the eerie feeling that he was facing a stranger.

"Your eyes . . . ," he could not resist blurting out.

"Oh, my, you haven't seen me without my contacts, have you? I'm thankful every day for those lenses, and the tinted ones really make a difference, don't they? Of course, my professor looks scholarly in his dark-rimmed glasses."

She put her arms around him and, holding herself close to him, whispered her second good night. Thoughts of all the nights to come were in her warm glance as she slipped from the room and gently closed the door.

"Tomorrow will be washed fresh and clean," she promised softly from the hall.

Jason stretched on the bed, on top of the covers, moving his back against the unaccustomed firmness. It seemed to him that the odor of violets ("fading violets"?) saturated the fabric of his pajamas, and for a few moments he fought off nausea.

He turned off the bedside lamp and lay in darkness except when lightning scooped away a patch near the window. The drumming of the rain and the roaring of distant thunder conjured up an eminently desirable world that called out to him invitingly.

Suddenly a pain such as he had never before experienced gripped at his chest and arms as with giant steel claws. He groped at himself in terror, feeling wetness gush from every pore. Even in his agony, a new something pervading the room caused him to raise his head from the pillow.

Surely Myrtle was not baking bread at this time of night— and especially on *this* night! But there was no mistake about the aroma of warm yeast filling the air.

"Martha." He could not tell whether the name constituted a question or a statement.

"Jason, you'd better come with me now." As ever, Martha's voice was not accusing, only accepting—tolerating and loving.

"Am I being foolish again?" he asked weakly, not making the effort to open his eyes, but seeing nonetheless.

"You've been carried away by a pair of brown eyes again, and we can't have you falling into a trap you won't be able to escape. Come along with me, Jay."

Only Martha had ever called him that. He breathed deeply, and there was no more pain. His knuckles relaxed, and his arms fell to his sides. From his peaceful face was reflected complete security.

Catching the Light

Armistice

*H*alfway down the aisle of Shiloh Church, Kate paused to lean on her cane, catch her breath, and look around. The dimness of the sanctuary always made her dizzy at first. Shiloh tried too hard to be a city church, she often thought. Nothing like little Walnut Grove, where you could hear the bees buzzing and the doves hollering—not to mention the shrill singing of the Methodists across the country road.

And she couldn't get used to those stained-glass windows that shut out the sun and the rain and the sight of limbs that told the season as they waved and dipped toward the ground and the quiet little community of low and tall monuments.

She felt a warm hand on the back of her arm and recognized the soft voice that said her name. "I'm sure glad you felt like coming out today, Miss Kate. It doesn't seem right when you're not in your place."

Ruby Jean walked her the rest of the way down to the second row of red theater chairs and helped her get settled into her aisle seat. She could always count on Ruby Jean.

How many times had she wished that those young fellows had been wise enough to appoint Ruby Jean's husband to the eldership instead of Ollie Mae's husband, Odie. Why, that poor man didn't know a thing to do till somebody told him.

Kate set her purse on the seat next to hers, with her tithe check tucked into a side pocket. Then she felt around for the right place to lay her cane so that she could begin to put her plan into action.

She thought to herself, *all right, little gentleman, come on and take your lesson!*

As the sanctuary gradually filled, Kate listened to the increasing titters and raised voices that preceded the opening of the morning service. She twisted a little in her somewhat snug seat and adjusted her skirts. A tiny breeze faintly scented with her liniment wafted to her nose. She nodded to all who paused to speak, patting the shoulders of some who bent close to her ear to speak a few words.

"Sister Kate, you didn't let the threat of rain scare you off," said Brother Vic in his loud preaching voice, reaching for her gloved hand.

"Oh, yes, I always have pain, but I've learned just to grit my teeth," she answered to his back as he slowly made his way up the aisle toward the pulpit.

Now, everybody, just leave me alone, she thought with the fervency of a prayer. She needed to concentrate on the coming of Wilbur Floyd.

Of course, it was Wilbur's mama who had the most need for a lesson, and Kate had been planning to tell Ollie Mae some things that would do her good. Why, right this minute, she was standing near the front, shifting her weight from one spike heel to the other, touching a gloved finger to one of the pink peony-like flowers that weighed down the broad straw brim that shaded more than half of her face.

Showing off another new hat, Kate observed, giving a fond pat to her own old but still good gray felt. Ollie Mae was the only woman in Shiloh church with a hat on, except for the older ones like Kate. It made her stand out, all right, no question about that. Ollie Mae liked to be noticed.

Kate leaned forward just far enough to see that her cane was perfectly situated. Usually she held on to it until services began, clutching the shiny silver knob between her white gloves. At least, she had done that since the day Wilbur Floyd shot up the aisle like a cyclone, grabbed her cane, mounted it like a stick horse, and rode it recklessly toward the rear of the sanctuary.

When Ollie Mae had finally hushed talking long enough to notice, she grabbed the boy, pried the cane from his grasp, then poked it toward Kate, glaring as if the child had been forced to make a horse out of her cane!

That was the beginning of undeclared war. Every Sunday, the door on the right side of the pulpit would burst open and children would erupt forth into the sanctuary, happy to be escaped from basement classrooms after a trying hour of relative inactivity. Out of the sea of bare legs and stiff butterfly dresses would emerge Wilbur Floyd with the clear intention of capturing Kate's cane again.

Every single time, she would pretend to ignore him while holding on with such force that her bad shoulder throbbed. At last, he would give up the futile wrestling match and, without ever appearing to recognize Kate's existence, rejoin other children bent on avoiding hands reaching out to snatch them and pin them down for yet another hour.

But today was going to be different. Kate couldn't recall a time when she had looked forward to anything with such pleasurable anticipation. She could feel the approach of unseen feet clopping toward her. The soles of her own feet tingled with the clamor of their coming, and her elbows were weak where they rested on the arms of her seat. It was all she could do to force her hands to remain folded on her Bible, which betrayed a slight trembling in her knees.

There they were at last, flooding the aisle, shoving, dropping papers, grabbing at each other, and studiously avoiding their parents' eyes. Wilbur Floyd, accomplished beyond his four years at getting his way, had materialized at Kate's elbow before she spied him, in spite of her watchfulness.

He stared in disbelief at her empty hands. His saucer-round brown eyes were Ollie Mae's made over. His face was usually blank except for a purposed gleam in his eyes, but now there was a definite spark of surprise, which almost immediately turned to delight when the shine of black metal against green carpet caught his attention. The coveted cane lay invitingly on the edge of the aisle.

Wilbur Floyd paused beside Kate and stared into her face. For the first time since the beginning of their intimate but wordless acquaintance, she returned his gaze, determined to keep her own face as expressionless as his.

Suddenly, he stooped, and stubby fingers tinged with streaks of red and yellow water colors reached hungrily toward the shining knob. But Kate was ready. A substantial dress oxford planted itself firmly atop the cane, and she shifted forward in her seat just enough to place her right shoe beside it as solid reinforcement.

The child stared in amazement, first at her feet and then up into her face, which she bent close to him.

"No," she sternly said, looking straight into the chubby, shrewdly innocent face which never failed to remind her of the picture on a Karo syrup can.

He reeled backward until he could lean against the seat directly across the aisle and, crouching in safety, send her looks burning with accusation. His lower lip began to tremble, and his chin dropped onto the top of his blue overalls bib.

"Mmmamma," he began to wail, with a sound which drowned out other noises and caused heads to turn. Kate could feel people wondering what on earth.

She settled her skirts and her books in readiness for the worship service and the sermon. Now, Brother Vic, Kate thought with some satisfaction, let's see what kind of lesson *you* can bring.

Kate felt a tentative tap on her shoulder, and she looked up with her smile ready. It was Ollie Mae, with a firm hold on Wilbur

Floyd's wrist but with no sign that she was aware what she was clutching. Kate wondered what had happened to her prissiness all of a sudden. It was as if she could see right through the thick coat of fancy makeup to a simple little girl who was begging for—what?

"Miss Kate. Did you know that my poor little Roscoe may be sent overseas?"

Kate certainly did know. For weeks Ollie Mae had been telling anybody who would listen. How could she have failed to know? She merely nodded, waiting for the rest that was bound to come. While she waited for Ollie Mae to continue, she watched a fat tear, brown with mascara, start to carve a track down Ollie Mae's cheek.

"Miss Kate, how did you stand it when your boys were away in the war and —got wounded, and all?"

Wounded and all? Kate felt her back stiffen. Did Ollie Mae dare to think that their circumstances were alike? Was she expected to sympathize with this silly crybaby?

She turned a little so that she could look Ollie Mae straight in the eye. She cleared her throat and gave her advice, plain and simple. "I stood it simply because I had to. Just like you will."

With mixed feelings, she heard the sternness in her own voice and was jarred by the force of every distinct syllable she had uttered. Ollie Mae must have felt it too, for she stepped back and flinched as if she had been slapped. She had expected something different, but she had been handed what was good for her. The truth.

Without another word, Ollie Mae snatched Wilbur Floyd's arm and dragged him to their row behind Kate, who suddenly felt drained. Her hand shook as she shuffled through her hymnal to find the announced page.

Kate could barely make out Brother Vic's words. The subject of the sermon was, "Who Is My Neighbor?"

She decided that she could think about that later, when she was at home in her own chair, reading from her big, well-marked Bible.

As Brother Vic proceeded through the points of his sermon, Kate's head was flooded with memories stirred by Ollie Mae's question. Looking straight ahead with her eyes turned toward the speaker, she relived the darkest, longest nights of her life, nights when the messages were brought from the government, followed by droves of well-meaning relatives and friends groping for ways to share helplessness and filling up smothering silences with ineffectual words.

Three gray monuments, beyond these stained glass windows that blocked her view, had silently endured the passing decades, brushed by the lowest of the dipping branches. To her alone they spoke unceasingly of the two whose bodies were shipped back after endless months of waiting and of one whose remains yet lay in some unknown corner of the world.

After the service had concluded, Kate waited for the crowd to clear out a little. She scanned the back of the room and was relieved to find no Ollie Mae in sight.

It was in the middle of the following week that Ruby Jean called to check on her and report the news that Roscoe had been injured.

"It was a wreck that happened when they were on maneuvers," Ruby Jean explained. "Of course, Ollie Mae's fit to be tied. It's what she's been scared to death of the whole time, although she was dreading trouble breaking out overseas somewhere."

"My lands," Kate said when the phone was back on its hook. "Why, Roscoe could've got hurt right here at home, in the hayfield, maybe. Driving a Jeep. My lands."

For most of that afternoon, Kate sat with her hands folded on the pages of the ragged-edged Bible, staring through the picture window without focusing on anything. Only vaguely did she register the passing of the mail car with its light flashing, the lumbering yellow school bus making its way into Shiloh to take on its loud, tired load. She couldn't collect her thoughts well enough to read her chapters or even to rest her head on the tall chair back and take a nap.

Her mind insisted on reaching back, far back, before she left Walnut Grove with her little boys and her new husband, the boys' daddy, leaving in Walnut Grove her own family—and a grave. Percy and she had been married only a few months when he had gone off to fight in the first big war. He was put on a big ship headed for the place where the battles were going on. Only he never got there.

It was only a month after he rode the train and went away from her that Laura, her sister, heard the bad news on her way home from school. She ran all the way so that she could be the first to tell. Kate was in the low loft over the corn crib, sorting out seed potatoes to plant.

"Sister, Sister! They're saying that Percy died on that boat. He took pneumonia, and a bunch of others did too. That man has a wire." She pointed over her shoulder toward a man who was just appearing around the corner of the house, humped over on a drab-looking horse.

Kate had been standing at the loft opening, staring at Laura in stunned silence. Then, before the tall man in the dark suit could slide down from the horse, she let out a wordless moan and jumped eight feet to the ground below.

Later she was told that everybody expected her to die, and they were sure that her and poor dead Percy's baby would be born dead. But for many days she lived to keep her anger alive, and then she went on to show the world her strength.

Most people speculated that Ollie Mae would not be at church on the Sunday after Roscoe's accident, but Kate leaned on her cane and waited beside her seat. When the basement door flew open to allow the children to spill out, Ollie Mae was with them, clutching the hand of an obviously subdued Wilbur Floyd, whose eyes were bigger and browner than ever.

The eyes of the two women met across the space separating them, and it was as if they were alone in the room—in the world. Ollie Mae stopped beside Kate without once averting her gaze.

Her face seemed naked without the usual makeup, and her brown head was small and vulnerable-looking without her customary hat.

What the older woman saw, in spite of herself, was a real human being wrestling with the kind of fear and suffering that she knew as well as she knew the geography of her own face.

Why, she looks like me, Kate thought, feeling silly at the very idea. For the first time, she saw some hope for Ollie Mae. She might be all right, after all, once some of that foolishness wore off.

They reached for each other at the same moment and accepted the shared embrace without a word. Kate felt tears on her cheek, part of them from Ollie Mae's eyes. The two clung to each other as if neither could stand without the other's support.

"Miss Kate! Miss Kate!"

Kate heard Wilbur Floyd and vaguely thought that she was surprised at the child's even knowing that she had a name. He began to jerk at the hem of her jacket and to pound on her hip insistently as if to punctuate his words. Kate glanced down at him from his mother's shoulder.

"Miss Kate, I learned mine. I can say it!" he almost yelled, totally triumphant. "I know my verse! It's 'Jesus wept'!"

The Four Hundred Ninety-first Time

*E*ven as she began to shift sleep-numbed limbs between smooth sheets in tentative exploration, it came to Maud that this was the day: on this day she would face, and squeeze within her grasp, that moment for which she had lived, almost, for so many months. The very awareness overwhelmed her, and she was engulfed in what was like a veritable Annunciation, replete with flaming torches and blaring trumpets. The unspeakable sight and sound assailed her still lidded eyes and muffled ears.

Today, she would confront Alice, constantly erring Alice, with indisputable documentation and—oh, the greatest wonder of it all!—with full divine sanction. All a-flush with righteous indignation, she would stand before her and declare to her that the limit of "seventy times seven" had now been reached, and Maud would be under no constraint to forgive her again, ever. Did not the Lord Himself set forth the guidelines? And had not Maud been scrupulously honest in her computations?

Reluctantly Maud extracted herself from her warm cocoon and sat, quite still, for a few moments on the side of the bed. She groped, almost frantically, among the soft, dark corners of her deepest self to find the beginnings of triumph which she had so long enjoyed in foretaste. Instead, she discovered crouching there the ragged specters of eroded certainties, the reaching tentacles of—*self*-doubt?

She felt a trembling begin, and a weakness. It was as though her body had actually participated in strength-sapping dreams through which she had labored the night away—dreams the likes of which she had willed from her secure being decades ago. Their return in past months had frightened her and undermined the very stature which she recognized as *herself* and equated with her sure sense of rightness.

Even in her dreams Maud seemed to know that the coming spring would be different from any of the fifty-four she had experienced before. She dreamed the dreams that used to haunt her in her waiting, striving years. She climbed trestles that did not quite make connections, leaving yawning spaces of air over which she somehow dared to leap, astounded at her own temerity. She dreamed of swimming desperately in black, annihilating waters while a part of her stood back and objectively assumed and accepted certain destruction. She thought she awakened and fought helplessly to pry open eyes which refused to come unglued. She felt the pounding of her heart and then really awakened to hear its actual beating in remembered terror and in relief that she could open her eyes and see the beginnings of light seeping through lace curtains at her east window and the outlines of familiar pink roses enclosed in egg-shaped designs marching in regular lines up and down twilight-toned walls.

Resisting an impulse to don her Sunday clothes in celebration of this day of days, Maud, still enveloped by a soft, insulating other-worldness, sat in her rocker and pulled on plain stockings and shoes, stretching the laces tight to make a secure bow knot. Then she moved across the dim hall to splash water from the cold faucet over her face and rub briskly with a fresh towel smelling of yesterday's timid young sun.

As she straightened before the mirror to brush out her iron-gray hair and shape it into a neat bun at the nape of her neck, she thought of Alice, still sleeping in the room adjoining her own. She raised her elbows to secure the bun with firm jabs of several pins. Out of the habit of years, from rote rather than from the heart, she told herself that she was thankful that her hair did not leap out in impossible little vines as Alice's did. Of course, Alice's hair could be more decent if she cared enough to tame it into submission instead of allowing it to stand out like a fuzzy halo around her chubby and usually perspiring face. Maud was convinced that outward order both bespoke and encouraged inward order, and Alice's obvious unconcern had always inflamed Maud's mind with such righteous indignation that she was barely able to countenance her presence, much less treat her with civility.

Maud deliberately reiterated in her mind some of Alice's most outlandish deeds, hoping to stir in herself the warmth of feeling appropriate for the occasion.

Her hand made little slippery, sucking sounds on the polished banister as she descended to the kitchen to prepare breakfast. Running water into the coffee pot, she peered out over her African violets atop the window sill and was pleased to see petunias covering the window box with tender new blooms. The sun and the sparkling dew bedazzled her eyes.

A flutter began at the bottom of Maud's stomach. She disliked seeing her hands tremble a little as she reached for a bowl and began to break eggs for her and Alice's breakfast. She thought of the flowerbeds as they had been when Alice came: rows of reds and whites in precise alternation all the way from the front steps to the mailbox. And the porch boxes and window boxes too Maud had planned carefully to present perfect pictures of color combinations. To her horror, Alice would flit out before breakfast, gown tail dragging across the dew-wet grass, and like as not come in with hands full of blooms stripped without regard to whatever pattern she had completely obliterated.

Such blatant unconcern for propriety and order was the very thing which Maud found most difficult to forgive. In fact, it was about Alice and flowers in particular—and her invasion of her life, in general—that Maud had been thinking on that Sunday morning over two and a half years ago, when she had arrived at the decision which had given shape to her life up to this unique day.

Once breakfast was finished and dishes washed and put away (every small detail was yet vivid in Maud's mind), she began the customary initial preparations for Sunday lunch. She peeled potatoes and left them in a pan of water ready for boiling, then laid two places on the yellow mats she always took from the top buffet drawer to use on Sunday if there were to be no guests. Alice, wiping her hands, mumbled that she was going to see about . . . something and went out the back door, leaving an unfinished sentence dangling in the air behind her as she so often did, to Maud's great frustration. Maud busied herself in the kitchen putting things back where they belonged, moving a chair so that its back was against the wall exactly half-way between the refrigerator and the pie safe, reaching for the sugar bowl on top of the refrigerator and setting it on the shelf over the stove where she had instructed Alice at least fifty times it should be kept.

Next she walked through the dining room to the parlor— Mama's room, she still called it, though her mother had been dead for twenty years—and immediately pulled the cord to slant the blinds so that the room was restored to its habitual solemn semi-darkness. Alice insisted on throwing open the blinds and letting in the light, little caring if the rug faded and everything in the room showed up as common.

Maud went over to the piano and shut the lid over the keys, using her sleeve to rub off some fingerprints. She closed the book that Alice had been using and placed it with the others inside the seat. Alice didn't—*wouldn't*—understand how *disrespectful* her playing was; she just marveled that the old instrument still sounded so good, except for one or two low keys, and she laughingly said she didn't like many tunes that called for them, anyway.

In those few moments while Alice was puttering around outside somewhere and Maud was left alone inside her empty house, she realized anew how much she missed being able to organize her own life and her own activities, how much harder it had become to deal even with simple things since Alice had come. She should have guessed at the devastation she would inflict, just by looking at the letter she had sent to request permission to live with her—full of fragments and spidery lines that climbed up and down the page, utterly disregarding margins.

Of course, she had known Alice for years, going back to the many summers she had spent with her family here in this very house. She remembered how, as a child two years older than herself, Alice had flouted all the rules Maud's mother imposed on her own children, causing them both to fall into disfavor by leading her off on jaunts without permission or making them late in returning home. Yet, Alice had remained a favorite of Maud's mother, her dear "Cousin Virgie" (who was not Alice's cousin at all—she and Alice's mother simply having been close childhood friends); and she was always warmly invited to return for the next summer vacation. All of Shiloh came to expect her.

So Maud, in spite of grave misgivings and complete unwillingness to risk the safe order of her comfortable life, had to say yes and allow Alice to come into her house. The months following her invading Maud's life, with sacks and boxes and a few pieces of authentic but disreputable luggage, had made all prior misgivings fade into nothingness in the face of reality.

After glancing around the parlor and satisfying herself that its proper state was restored, Maud mounted to her room to dress for church. She turned to look at the clock which ticked loudly from its place atop her bureau, and she thought with irritation that Alice was staying out in the yard or wandering in the woods on purpose to make them late for church: it was ten minutes before nine, and they always left at ten past nine in order to have time to walk the short distance down the country road to the little white building and get settled in their pew before someone else took it. She was beginning to be really angry as she completed her toilet, smoothing the skirt of her dark rayon print and placing her black felt hat so as not to mash her hair out of place. After Labor Day she always wore her black hat, purse, and shoes regardless of whether summer weather persisted. She opened her glove drawer and removed freshly washed white gloves, which she put in her purse ready to wear after locking the front door. She wouldn't risk getting them soiled.

As she descended the stairs, she heard Alice in the kitchen, talking to herself and splashing water. When she reached the door and looked in, she could not believe her eyes. There at the cabinet stood Alice punching a last branch of red foliage into a vase among tall white arrow-shaped flowers. She stepped back to survey her work with obvious approval and then looked glowingly at Maud.

At first Maud could not say a word. Then she shoved Alice out of the way to crane her neck so that she could see her fall flower bed—what was left of it, a ragged mockery for the world to see. She ran to the dining room window to see better what it made her sick to see at all. She shouted back to Alice, still standing in the kitchen with her hands embracing the round belly of the vase.

"I planted those whippoorwill flowers and those fire-bushes out there by the rail fence so they'd show up white, red, white, red, and high, low, high, low, for people coming and going along the road to appreciate. I tended them and I put pine shavings around them, and you go right out there and ruin them in a minute! This is all I can take."

She slammed her purse down on the dining room table and strode over to the door to glare at Alice.

"But, Maudie. . . . " She clutched the vase harder and sounded breathless. "Maudie, I thought you heard what I was going to do. I just imagined poor little Miss Minnie Corbitt might enjoy looking at them during the sermon. Bless her soul, she can't hear a word Brother Malvyn says, even from the second pew. I'm really sorry, Maudie."

"My name is *Maud*, and *I'm* going to church. *You* can come or not, as you please." She went through the dining room to grab up her purse and leave through the front door, slamming the screen resoundingly behind her.

Her feet moved her along their habitual path without her being aware of her progress or of her surroundings. A short distance ahead of her moved a little cluster of people, but she did not catch up with them until she entered the churchyard. She merely nodded to the few who caught her eye and passed into the dim building, making her way down the short aisle until she came to her accustomed pew, the third on the left.

Behind her the crowd gathered with its usual subdued whispering and shuffling. The Reverend Malvyn was already making his way down the aisle, shaking hands along the way, when Alice rushed in. Maud kept her back straight and her neck stiff, but a few rows behind her Brother Malvyn spoke: "Well, Sister Rucker, you certainly don't have an empty hand to offer me this morning. Did you rob a greenhouse?"

Alice's answer escaped Maud's ears, but down the aisle she came, bearing her floral tribute right up to the front corner, where she carefully balanced it on the three-legged stand which always stood there for that very purpose but which was usually empty except in spring or after a funeral. She straightened one of the whippoorwill spikes and, apparently unself-conscious, tipped her head to one side to take a final close-up look of approval. Her hat, precariously mounted in her hurried departure from home, almost slipped off, and she used both hands to pull it more firmly into place as she made quick, short steps back to squeeze past Maud into their pew, her pale blue voile brushing against Maud's dark knees. Her face was now flushed, partly from rushing and partly from realizing that she was under the scrutiny of the assembly; and damp sprinkles of baby-yellow hair stood out around the edge of her white straw pillbox.

"You could at least have worn gloves," Maud whispered, keeping her neck stiff and looking straight ahead. "Especially with that unsightly walnut stain all over your hands. Everybody must have noticed when you straightened the Ward plaque."

Alice spread her hands wide in her lap and looked at the up-turned palms as if surprised, then at Maud's white gloves primly folded on top of a maroon hymnal. "Oh. Well, . . . maybe they'll forgive me when we share the Christmas goodies." But as she reached into the rack for a hymnal, she glanced sidewise at Maud with a certain question in her eyes.

Just as the minister and Brother Albert, the music director, were seating themselves in identical chairs on either side of the pulpit and an elderly gentleman assigned to deliver the invocation was shuffling onto the platform, the unmistakable voice of Miss Minnie interrupted the silence. "They haven't started yet, Son. We're in good time."

Her stroke-deepened voice, unheard by her own deaf ears, caused the few visitors who didn't know her to glance around in surprise. Her young grandson's whispered answer encouraged her to be quiet as he led her down to the second pew and helped her to lower her stiff, frail body into her corner spot by the aisle. With scarlet face lowered into his collar, the boy sped to the back of the sanctuary to join his smirking peers.

Once the invocation was finished, Miss Minnie turned partway around, curious to see who was in attendance, and Alice began to nod vigorously and point toward the front corner on Miss Minnie's right. Finally Miss Minnie's pale eyes lighted on Alice; then she turned with several others whose rambling eyes had also observed Alice's gestures. The old woman peered for several moments toward the vase of flowers and then, with a brief glance over her shoulder to bestow a slow-spreading watery smile of appreciation upon Alice, shifted her body to face the front corner for the duration of the service.

As always, Maud conscientiously put her total being into participating in all of the parts of the worship service. She was moved by thoughts of the goodness of God, but something there was in her that responded with an almost frenzied awe and delight before an awareness of His strictness. Sometimes she whispered to herself, "Behold the goodness and the *severity* of God," and then she would tremble. For this was an attribute she could understand and appreciate—and deal with, she thought. When she meticulously obeyed the clearly written laws engraved on the pages of the Word, she experienced a real satisfaction in the knowledge that God's hunger for submission on the part of His creatures was being fed and that His severity was for the time diverted from her as helpless object. An especially keen sense of security and wholeness came to her when she responded to one of the "Thou shalt nots" as if the admonition were a sharp, clean knife slicing away diseased flesh to leave a healthy body. Sitting before Brother Malvyn, always applying text and commentary to her own particular case, she felt, not pride, but a measure of safety in knowing that she had done—or refrained from doing— those things throughout her adult life.

It was into this haven which Maud had carefully constructed for herself that Alice had come, and it was this sense of order and well-being that she had disrupted. She was like a rock or a pebble tossed into the middle of a glassy stream, causing ripple on ripple on ripple to circle outward and distort all reflections. She was an intrusive bird, constantly fluttering at the window of Maud's life, beating frenetic wings against dark, ominous panes, fanning and beating off any possibility of rest.

"Exactly like a silly little blue bird," Maud thought as Alice leaned forward to place a finger on the round pink cheek of an infant whose wide fixed stare over his mother's shoulder shifted briefly in response. Attempting to transmit her disapproval through a stiffening of her body and light tapping of a white index finger on the front of her hymnal, Maud made fierce internal adjustment and succeeded in wrenching her attention back to the speaker. He had put on spectacles to read from a New Testament held before his face at arm's length.

"Then came Peter to him, and said, 'Lord, how oft shall my brother sin against me, and I forgive him? till seven times?' Jesus saith unto him, 'I say not unto thee, Until seven times: but, until seventy times seven.'" As he closed his book, Maud felt that Brother Malvyn was looking at her and her alone.

Her reaction was so violent that she glanced self-consciously around, certain that her face must betray the burning flush that she could feel suffusing her whole body. She had been asking how long she must continue to submit to Alice's lawlessness and her chaotic influence, how long before she might declare an acceptable end to her patience, and now the answer had been given to her in just the concrete, finite terms that might give structure and order back to the nights and days of her existence.

The infinite and the mysterious had always frightened Maud: she could handle—and, in a way, possess—only what she could measure or count. As a child she had known exactly how many pencils were standing, sharp points up, in the jelly jar on her desk. Now she could tell precisely how many dahlia bulbs lined the garden fence, how many tomato plants had comprised the straight green rows or how many bunches of onions were hanging from nails on the tool shed wall. Though she never failed automatically to count her precious pieces of Carnival Glass when tenderly giving them their monthly bath, she already knew the number beforehand. And what if Providence, knowing her better than she knew herself, intending to test her and to straighten her propensity to forgive, was offering her, for her own soul's sake, this way to restore order and to bear what seemed unbearable?

Absent-mindedly, Maud stood to mouth with the rest of the congregation the words to the closing hymn: "Though your sins be as scarlet, they shall be as white as snow." Her mind was reaching toward the acceptable means of dealing with the sins of others who, in their perversity, lacked her burning desire to comply with the Will and the Way.

Following the benediction she spoke to those who spoke to her as the crowd shifted slowly toward the open door where the Reverend Malvyn stood shaking hands and greeting each parishioner, bending to pat the heads of the very young. Maud dutifully inquired of one or two regarding the health of ailing family members, trying hard to heed the answers.

Most of the adults were in clusters chatting as she crossed the yard taking the direction of home. She noted Alice accompanying Miss Minnie and the grandson, who had his gangling arms wrapped around Maud's flower vase, to the family car. Though the two women usually walked to church together, Maud nearly always was out of her Sunday church clothes and into the second-best dress and shoes she reserved for Sunday afternoon wear before Alice came bubbling in, with items to share about neighborhood goings-on—gossip, Maud labeled it.

Throughout the afternoon and evening of that most memorable Sunday of Maud's life, the activities were routine, but she felt an excitement and an anticipation that were almost sickening. In her room at last, once she had dressed for bed and loosed her thick hair so that it hung almost to her waist, she pulled her rocking chair nearer the bedside lamp and began to read from the Bible. Over and over she read Matthew 18, and then she closed the book upon her forefinger and sat with eyes tightly shut, her lips occasionally moving in supplication. At first she was aware of Alice moving about in the adjoining room. But long before she closed the Bible and slipped into bed, the whole house was still, filled with a silence that seemed to be waiting and watching.

The morning was gray when she arose and quietly, but decisively, descended to the kitchen. A calendar hung on the pantry door, and to this Maud went straightway. She had ripped off the top sheet and was turning when she heard a sound behind her.

"Well, Maud, I've always heard the one who turns the calendar to the new month gets to rule the household, so I guess you win." Alice stood in the backdoor, laughing. An old sweater was buttoned over her gown, and her hair stood in damp ringlets all around her face. Maud hated the quiver that she could not keep out of her voice as she asked, "Have you completely lost your mind, wandering around out there in the dark?"

"Oh, it's not really dark," Alice said, bending to pull a burr from her hem. "The fog is so marvelous. A while ago I thought that old beech stump by the pasture gate was a dog—or maybe a wolf!" She laughed again.

Wordlessly Maud turned and climbed to her room. Her hands were trembling, and she sat looking at the front of the calendar page several minutes before she felt calm enough to write. At the top of the sheet, above the thirty squares into which the time called September had been neatly parceled, was a bright picture of a forest of orange and yellow leaves being tossed by the wind, whose invisible presence the artist had skillfully managed to suggest. Under the picture, in large black letters, were the words "Destroyer and Preserver." Near the bottom of the sheet was a recipe for wild-grape wine.

Finally she turned to the clean, white side of the sheet and, resting it on the smooth cover of an old album, slowly and carefully wrote from memory two verses, underlining with her pen the words *seventy times seven*. Then she arose and went over to pull out the glove drawer at the top of the bureau. She moved her five pairs of white gloves to one side, smoothly stacked with the short ones on top, to make room for the sheet to lie flat on the bottom of the drawer. She laid her pen beside it, ready for use.

From that day forward, she was careful never to make a mark on the record sheet until she was convinced in her heart that she had forgiven Alice, for the computation was, after all, not of Alice's misdeeds—the Lord would keep an account of them—but of her own mental and spiritual triumphs, which she trusted that the Lord was also noting on some great Page of His awareness.

Throughout that first winter the record sheet received many entries; by Christmas a long line of tallies marched to the very margin like soldiers bound in groups of four—or unwilling convicts chained about their waists. The number *seventy times seven* had in the beginning seemed to Maud so exaggerated that it was difficult to imagine that even Alice could ever place herself in need of forgiveness so many times as that. But she soon came to understand that it was the small, ostensibly insignificant deeds that were the most dangerous threats to her own peace and assurance—that were being sent, indeed, to try her to the limit. So the tallies multiplied, although in the first months—and sometimes later—there were long waits between the deed and the black token of forgiveness. Sometimes several marks denoting later cases were inscribed before Maud was able, with a sigh, finally to take up her pen and with a firm movement of the wrist aver that once more a spiritual battle had been fought and won.

Yet in those times there was little danger that her computations would become confused or inaccurate, for when she opened the drawer to make an entry, she could easily tell over the occasion for each mark. At one glance she could pick out a particularly heavy mark, a cross tally, which reminded her of the day Alice had been reading from Mama's old book of Tennyson's poetry. She had actually brought the book out of the parlor and into the dining room to read some lines from "Locksley Hall: Sixty Years After" to Maud, who was on her knees mending the seat cover of one of the dining chairs. She suddenly stopped reading, and Maud glanced up to see, in horror, that the back of the fragile book had broken in two, and Alice was standing with half in each hand. Alice's obvious remorse did not speed the bestowal of forgiveness.

Sometimes Maud wondered whether Alice had the Lord's forgiveness even though she had given hers. For example, February of that first winter was unusually bitter and ferocious, and Maud relied on supplies she had laid by for such an eventuality, leaving the house only to lumber and slide down the road for worship services. On one Sunday morning Alice announced that she would not be accompanying Maud to church, indicating that she felt the beginnings of a head cold.

Nevertheless, the first thing that Maud saw upon returning from church was Alice's galoshes, sitting on the kitchen floor surrounded by a spreading pool of melted snow. She was warming her hands over a lighted stove eye, and with no apparent feelings of guilt she explained that she had decided to run across the pasture to take old Mr. Totty some hot chicken soup in a thermos. After a time of struggling, Maud made herself forgive Alice for misrepresenting the truth to her; regarding her failure to attend worship services, she would have to deal with the Lord.

By the end of the first year, when a new September arrived with its stripping winds, three hundred marks lay like slits on the paper inside the glove drawer. When she opened the drawer to make an entry or to take out or return her gloves on Sunday, her eyes were assailed and astonished by the sight. She could still envision the end toward which she firmly marched with them, though not as clearly and not nearly as frequently as when she first conceived the plan. At first, although only a few marks were made, she could already hear herself coldly announcing to a shocked Alice that the moment had arrived: that the Lord no longer would require her to endure the intolerable. She would suggest, kindly but immovably, that Alice take her things and go to Akron, to live with a *real* cousin. Whether she moved there or elsewhere would not be Maud's concern; her own hands and heart would be clean. She avidly pictured Alice and her cluttered ragtag possessions piled around her in a taxi-cab ready to drive away and leave behind the uninterrupted flow of peace.

But as time went on, she thought less and less of the end. Sometimes it seemed to her that she preferred not to contemplate the end. She did notice that forgiveness came more easily and more speedily; though often, when she remembered to record just before retiring, it was difficult for her to be sure that accounts were as nearly complete as they used to be.

The second winter was even harder with respect to her record keeping task. The number had grown, and now several lines stretched across the sheet. She knew that a few more months were bound to bring her to her goal. Then, after Christmas, she came down with pneumonia and was seriously ill for the first time in her life. For days stretching into weeks she floated in and out of reality. Time was a fuzzy nonentity punctured but not logically divided by Alice's comings and goings, her hovering over the bed to add cover or to rest a cool hand on her burning forehead. When she was better but too weak to do more than move about in her room and then fall back into her rocking chair to rest, Maud looked at the sheet; and once more she even added, dutifully, light marks to designate forgiveness for a few infractions that were vague and inexact in her mind.

Before spring was more than a suggestion or a wish, Maud could feel its coming in stealth and promise. She told herself it was because of her illness that she tingled with yearning to be done with winter. When grass and new yellow leaves actually did appear, she could have laughed with gladness. At night she longed for morning; at dawn she almost ran to the window to try to slice through grayness to wonders shortly to be revealed. Moving noiselessly about, still partly in the dream world where she had climbed but not fallen, yet a little subdued by the desperate dream-fight with eyes that refused to open, she dressed as in a trance and then, before breakfast, went outside to seek new wonders. She was a self she did not know.

In the fall Alice had bought bulbs and secreted them in every unlikely place, so that now, every morning, where nothing—or mere brownness—had been the night before, a crocus laughed toward the sky, as though pleased to surprise. Or a daffodil leaped from behind a rock; a million grape hyacinths were suddenly nodding to each and all from the recesses of tree roots and fence corners.

Maud was certain that she had never been more miserable or more ecstatic than she was during that climactic spring. More than once she strongly suspected that she was losing her wits completely. But each blossom seemed to be taking root and strength and substance out of the depths of her very being. She could sense the vibrations of life-making forces running through the entire earth, and that trepidation became one with her very pulse beat. She wondered that Alice did not see and that their lives moved through outward routines with no discernible difference.

She could hardly breathe as she went to her room to make the last entry. An afternoon thunderstorm had risen and growled and spilled its life out, leaving behind a damp chill but also a deep-down freshness. Maud, looking into the parlor, noticed that beneath the window a dark circle marred the old figured rug, turning its pale red to black. Alice had forgotten to lower the window, which she insisted on opening almost every day, though Maud preferred to keep it closed and the blinds drawn under the lace curtains. Now she walked halfway across the room with the intention of closing it, then hesitated at the round center table, abstractedly removed some dust from a lamp base with her finger, changed her mind, and continued to her room.

After inscribing the final mark, she counted to make sure that no mistake was possible. Sure enough, there were ninety-eight groups of marks going across the sheet almost ten times. Maud looked at it for a long time. She saw dark lines and light lines, and then it was as if she saw no lines at all, but one haze refusing her eyes admittance. She could not tell how she felt in this moment that should have been perfectly familiar and entirely welcome. She was confused, and were not this confusion and uncertainty the very enemies which her God-sanctioned battle strategy had been intended to quell?

She took the sheet with her and went over to her chair. There she sat all night. A few times she dozed and, in her shallow sleeping, dreamed. Once more she was at that dizzying height that had become as familiar to her as the prosaic environs of her waking hours. She stood with one foot on a firm rung, the other dangling precariously over nothingness. Above, out of toe's reach, was the next rung. A quiet voice, which seemed far away and yet appeared to originate in her own head, said, "Have you forgotten that you have wings?"

When she awoke the last time, her right hand had been clutching the calendar sheet so tightly that it was wrinkled. Slowly and thoughtfully she straightened it before doubling it and tearing each part in half and then again, over and over until there were many fragments in her hands and on the floor around her feet. The pieces she picked up and threw into the grate were ragged white bits with tiny black lines like veins disconnected from the source of life.

"Finished," she whispered as she rose to her feet.

As she prepared breakfast, she was aware of waiting for something, she knew not what. Alice came down and was as usual. She chattered while they ate and cleared the table.

At the sink beginning to wash the dishes, Alice suddenly cried out. "Oh, Maudie, look, look!"

Maud put down the sugar bowl hurriedly and rushed to Alice's side. "What is it?"

"A hummingbird! Precious little thing. Just look!"

"Where?"

"There, there, in that tall petunia." She snatched a hand out of the water to point.

Suddenly there was a loud crash and a splattering of water, just as Maud finally saw the tiny bird lift its beak from the red tube and flit away.

At the same time she realized what it was that had happened.

"Oh, Maudie, your African violet—your beautiful Imperial. I knocked it off the sill. Oh, I'm so sorry!"

Stunned, Maud looked wordlessly into the sink full of suds. She looked at the empty window sill. She swallowed.

"I . . . I think I knocked it when I pulled the curtain back to look," Alice gasped, frantically feeling beneath the thick suds for the submerged flower.

"Here, Alice, let me do that; you'll cut your finger." Maud plunged her hand into the hot water. Soft, grainy dirt lined the bottom of the sink. She searched cautiously for the sharp fragments of the broken container.

"Get your hands out," she repeated. Her own hand searched to find Alice's. When she found it, it moved like a slippery fish within her grasp. Snowy piles of suds foamed above their wrists. Maud looked down and saw, rising to bob and float on the sparkling foam, tiny blood-red scraps of broken blossoms.